WHEN YOU'RE FINALLY HOME

SAGEBRUSH RANCH - BOOK 5

APRIL MURDOCK

Copyright © 2023 April Murdock and Sweet River Publishing

All rights reserved.

No part of this book may be reproduced in any form or by any electronic or mechanical means, including information storage and retrieval systems. Publisher expressly prohibits any form of reproduction.

This is a work of fiction. Any references to names, characters, organizations, places, events, or incidents are either products of the author's imagination or are used fictitiously.

∽

ISBN: 978-1-963187-04-5

Cover design by Erin Dameron-Hill

MORE FROM APRIL MURDOCK

Sagebrush Ranch

When You're Friends
When You're Waiting
When You're His Crush
When You're Competing
When You're Finally Home
When You're Fake Dating
When You're Enemies
When You're Keeping Secrets

Returning to Rocky Ridge

One Last Chance
Two Cowboy Promises
Three Times Charmed

Billionaire Ranchers Second Generation

Faking Her Engagement

Protecting His Heart
Marrying Her Friend
Dating Her Crush
Taking His Chance
Trusting Her Hero

The Brothers of Duncan Ranch

A Party Planner for the Cowboy
A Second Chance for the Cowboy
A Rare Beauty for the Cowboy
An Open Heart for the Cowboy
A Christmas Kiss for the Cowboy

Silverstone Dude Ranch

Cowboy's Redemption
Cowboy's Surprise
Cowboy's Competition
Cowboy's Fate
Cowboy's Challenge
Cowboy's Assumption
Cowboy's Myth
Cowboy's Rival
Cowboy's Destiny

Billionaire Ranchers Series

Impressing Her Billionaire Cowboy Boss
Keeping Her Billionaire Cowboy CEO
Saving Her Billionaire Cowboy Hero
Loving Her Billionaire Cowboy Partner
Arguing With Her Billionaire Cowboy

Teaching Her Billionaire Cowboy Rookie

The Brothers of Thatcher Ranch

The Cowboy's One and Only
The Cowboy's City Girl
The Cowboy's Troublemaker
The Cowboy's Second Chance

Wealth and Kinship

The Billionaire's Heart
The Billionaire's Hope
The Billionaire's Generosity
The Billionaire's Loyalty
The Billionaire's Sincerity
The Billionaire's Promise

Silverstone Ranch

The Movie Star Becomes a Cowboy
The Cowboy gets a Second Chance
The Chef Chases His Cowboy Dream
The Billionaire Tries the Cowboy Life
The Royal Cowboy Chooses Love

Texas Redemption

A Long Road Home for the Broken Ranger
Sweet Second Chances for the Reluctant Billionaire
New Inspiration for the Lonely Rockstar
A Change of Plans for the Youngest Son
A Rude Awakening for the Ambitious Ex-Boyfriend

Small Town Billionaires

The Billionaire's High School Reunion
The Aimless Billionaire
The Billionaire's Charity Date
The Beach Bum Billionaire
The Grouchy Billionaire
The Billionaire's Home Town

Christmas Miracles

Her Undercover Billionaire Boss
The Billionaire's Family Christmas
Christmas Carols for the Billionaire

WHEN YOU'RE FINALLY HOME

SAGEBRUSH RANCH - BOOK 5

APRIL MURDOCK

CHAPTER ONE

If this wasn't rock bottom, Katrina didn't know what was.

Everything in her life had been leading to one singular moment, and she'd lost. Now she was empty and exhausted with nothing to show for it.

What was someone in her position supposed to do when a dream was snatched right out from under her?

She sat cross-legged on her bed, clad in sweats and a tank top with her computer in her lap. The words on the screen blurred together.

The worst part was that she couldn't share just how depressed she was with anyone because no one understood. All four of her brothers had found their happiness —but that wasn't a surprise. They knew who they were and where they belonged.

Without her job in California, she felt lost.

That cold sensation of feeling like a complete failure was a constant companion. It wouldn't even leave for the few minutes a day she was forced to interact with people who had her best interests at heart.

Another condolence email filled her computer screen, informing her the company she'd sent her resumé to had decided to go in another direction. So another second interview that would never happen. Awsome.

She picked up the laptop and shoved it to the side, throwing herself back against the pillows and heaving a groan. If she couldn't even get a second interview with a company she was a perfect fit for, how was she going to find a way out of this forsaken town?

Rocky Ridge was great... for *some* people. But it wasn't meant for her.

Katrina loved her family and friends. Moving away from them had been the hardest part about wanting to leave the small town. But the undeniable truth was that she needed something more than this place had to offer.

It just appeared no one needed her.

She pressed the heels of her hands into her eyes and took a deep breath. No more tears. She refused to cry over this again. At this point, she'd been going through the motions for the sake of her family. She'd helped her brothers with the day-to-day ranch stuff, and she'd babysat her niece a couple of times. But none of it felt... *right*.

How could they expect her to come home from fast-paced jobs in New York and California where everything was bustling to a place like Rocky Ridge, where time moved slower than a turtle crossing the road?

Katrina leaned over, placing her elbows on her knees and her head in her hands. If she didn't find a new job soon, she was going to end up stuck in this tiny cowboy town with nothing to show for it.

A soft knock at the door drew her attention, causing her to lift her head right as it opened. In breezed Brianne with a grin on her face.

"Good news," she sang. "Jackson said he's willing to try again." Her splash of pink hair helped her stand out from the rest of the folks who lived in the more reserved community. She perched on the edge of Katrina's bed, pulling her legs beneath her, and glanced toward the door with her bright blue eyes. "Simon thinks you should do it, right, Simon?"

Katrina shifted her focus from one friend to the other. Simon stood in the doorway, almost the complete opposite of Brianne. He had dark brown hair and dark green eyes, and he was considerably more reserved in his looks.

Simon was one of the most optimistic people she'd ever met. There wasn't a bad experience he couldn't find a silver lining to. At times, his sunny disposition was unbearable—especially when Katrina wanted to wallow. But she had nothing to wallow about when it came to the circumstances of her life compared to his.

Simon leaned his broad shoulder against the doorjamb and crossed his arms, staring at her from beneath a worn cowboy hat. He gave her a crooked smile but didn't confirm what Brianne had said. In moments like this,

Katrina could appreciate his strong, silent personality. The last thing she needed was for Simon to guilt her into doing what was probably the right thing to do—and at the same time the one thing she had no intention of doing.

"I don't care if Jackson Duncan wants to take me on a date. I'm not going."

"Not like that you're not." Brianne gestured toward the sweats and the messy bun atop Katrina's head. "I don't even think Simon would take you out looking like that… and we both know *he's* not picky."

"Brianne!" Katrina gasped. "Be nice." She mouthed the word "sorry" to Simon, who shrugged.

Brianne snickered. "Relax. He knows I'm joking. If anyone here has a history of being picky, it's probably Simon. I don't remember the last time he went on a date." She shot one more look toward Simon and tilted her head. Her nose scrunched as if to show just how hard she was thinking about this particular situation. "When *was* the last time you went on a date, Simon?"

His gaze flitted to Katrina and back to Brianne. "I don't know. Last month?"

Brianne snorted. "If that were the case, I would have heard about it. You know my mother hears everything that goes on in this town. I can't remember, and clearly neither can you. Maybe we need to set you up on a date, too."

Katrina had to hold back a laugh that threatened to bubble up from her chest. It both hurt and felt amazing to finally find something to laugh about. She put a hand to her chest and grimaced.

"Don't make me laugh. It hurts to laugh so hard." She found Simon's eyes. "Don't worry, neither one of us has to go on a date with anyone. Relationships aren't the only thing that brings us purpose."

The look in his eyes caught her off guard. If she were reading into things, she would have thought he was hiding something from her. A secret girlfriend? No, Simon wouldn't keep something like that from them. Besides, he wasn't all that great at hiding things. One small grin and she knew he had something to tell her.

Brianne moved closer to her on the bed. "I know you've been down lately, but you have to trust me on this one. You need a change to get you out of this funk."

"I don't think a date is going to do that for me," Katrina muttered. "I don't care about dating. I don't want to have to think about what I'm wearing or how I'm acting. I just want to get my career back on track."

Brianne sighed. "I'm not telling you to stop applying. But people can sense when you're not feeling great. I'm telling you. They know when their applicant isn't happy. No one wants to hire a depressed employee."

"But I wouldn't be depressed if I had the job." Katrina glanced toward Simon in the doorway, pleading for him to back her up.

"So, it's a chicken and egg situation. The only thing that's going to help you is improving your mood. So get out there, distract yourself, and make those companies realize that you have other things going for you so they end up head-hunting you instead of you stalking them."

Katrina huffed as she pulled her knees to her chest and wrapped her arms around her legs. As much as she hated to admit it, her friend had made a good point. If what she was doing wasn't working, then there had to be a problem on her end.

Could it be so simple as her mood?

"Besides, Jackson isn't going to be around much longer. He's the perfect person to go on a date with because he'll be going home in two weeks." Brianne beamed, clearly happy with herself for finding someone Katrina wouldn't have to dump. "Once you get the first one out of the way, you can date more and then you'll be back to your happy self."

Simon chuckled from where he stood, drawing their attention. Brianne gave him a strange look, to which he chuckled again.

"Come on, Katrina has never been the peppy one. That's always been you, Brianne. And I'm the optimistic one. Out of the three of us, she's the planner and the serious one."

Brianne rolled her eyes and gave Katrina a flat look. "Don't listen to him. You're *happy*. Just a different kind of happy."

Simon was right and Katrina knew it. The funny thing was that she didn't realize he was such a people-watcher. While they'd been friends for what felt like an eternity, she would have never pegged him as being the kind of person to label anyone in their group.

She nodded to Brianne if only to put a stop to *that* conversation. Then she rubbed her nose into her knees before resting her chin there. "Okay, so I go on a date with Jackson. Then what? I'm not stupid enough to believe that one date is going to put me in a better mood. We had Daniel's wedding, and I was miserable even then. I just can't seem to get over this slump."

Brianne waved a hand through the air with a light laugh. "That's because you weren't taking my advice. Believe me, when I'm done with you, everything is going to be bright and shiny again." She got to her feet and flashed them a smile.

"Where are you going?" Katrina demanded. Her friend already looked like she was on a mission. While she probably shouldn't have asked a question she didn't want the answer to, Katrina still waited for confirmation.

"I'm going to call Sam and tell him that you're on board with going on a date with his cousin. Then I'm going to find someone I can go with so we can double." Before she left the room, Brianne patted Simon on the shoulder. "I don't suppose you'd want to go with me?"

Her tone was teasing, but it didn't stop him from grimacing.

"Pass," he muttered.

Brianne snickered. "I didn't think so. Do you want to go with us anyway? I can find—"

"I'm going to stop you right there. I'm taking on extra shifts at the Overlook Grand Resort so chances are slim that I'll even be available."

She pouted. "Well, you're no fun." She tossed one more grin toward Katrina. "I'll text you later when I have the details."

Katrina nodded again. She and Simon watched Brianne breeze out of the room and then Simon turned his attention to her. He finally moved into her room and sat on the edge of the bed.

"Sometimes I wonder how we all got to be friends."

She moved closer to him, swinging her legs over the edge. "Because you and I were besties and Brianne wanted to join in."

"We were only besties because of your parents. If they hadn't helped out when my grandparents started declining, I don't know what would have happened to me. To us, actually. Your mom was so generous to us."

Katrina's heart constricted. This was one of the reasons that she couldn't believe Simon was so happy all the time. He'd lost his mother when he was about five years old. His grandfather got dementia when he was in ninth grade and that was really hard on him and his grandmother. He'd had one of the hardest childhoods she could think of and yet he was still standing and one of the finest men she knew.

"I don't know, I think we would have been friends regardless." She rested her head on his shoulder.

"Maybe."

They sat in silence like they had a tendency to do. Mostly because she was too worried about how everything in her life was going and he was just a quiet contemplator.

Brianne was the one who couldn't stand silence, which was probably another reason she had loved being a part of their group—she didn't have to compete with anyone else when it came to filling the void.

"Do you really think I should go on a date with Jackson?"

Simon grunted.

"That doesn't answer my question."

"What I think shouldn't matter. It's how you feel that does."

"And that doesn't answer my question, either." She pulled away from him and stared up into his handsome face. "With what you know about me, what would you say?"

He shrugged. "You've never really been interested in relationships with people around here. The only guy I remember you having a thing for was back in New York."

She made a face. "Yeah, and we saw how that turned out. He was only dating me so he could take over my job." Katrina groaned. "I should have seen it coming. I can't believe I let him in like that."

"It's not your fault."

Katrina frowned. No, it wasn't her fault, but she should have known better than to open herself up to someone she worked with. Even she knew better than that and she'd let it happen anyway. That experience alone had shifted the way she viewed relationships. "Well, I guess if I have to go on a date with anyone, Jackson is a better fit. At least I don't have to worry about him taking over my job—because I don't have one to steal."

CHAPTER TWO

Beneath the light tone in Katrina's voice, Simon could hear the sadness. It was an ache that he couldn't fix, as much as he wished he could.

"Whatever you want to do, I'm here for you. You know that, right?"

Katrina shifted so she could rest her head on his shoulder again. "Yeah, I know. You've always been there for me when I needed you most."

Nothing was truer than that statement right there. Ever since he was a kid, parentless and alone, Katrina had been there for him, too. They'd formed a bond so tight that not even Brianne could come between it.

Their little group was close, but not as close as he was with this woman who sat beside him. Sometimes he wondered if Brianne could sense it, and if she felt like they'd edged her out. If so, she didn't show it.

"What do you think you'll do on your date?"

He asked the question quietly, fully admitting to himself that he didn't want to hear about it. Secretly, he didn't want her dating anyone either. He had a feeling that the second she found someone to love, he would lose the only person he considered his family.

And at the same time, he couldn't stand in her way. He had to be the support she needed without being the person who destroyed her future.

She took a deep breath and let it out. "I don't know. Frankly, I don't care. Brianne is being ridiculous. I don't need to spend time with a stranger to feel better."

"Then what would make you feel better?"

Katrina peeked up at him from where her cheek rested against his shoulder. "I just want to get out of here, you know? I want to be in the city again where everything keeps moving faster and faster. I need to feel that electricity—it fills me with energy and a sense of purpose like nothing else."

Once upon a time, that description would have hurt his feelings. He would have taken it personally that she didn't want to stick around in the town where they grew up—in the town where they had become friends.

But he knew better than to believe she was talking about him when she called this place dull. Whenever something big happened at work, he was the first person she'd call. And the same went for him. They were still connected even when she was far away.

"Yeah, I get that. But you have to admit that Brianne made a good point. You need to find purpose before you can try to sell yourself. It's like when you got that job in New York. You were confident and living life to the fullest. I think people can feel that in the emails you write and the phone interviews you take."

"I guess. I just wish I didn't have to fake it so much."

"So don't."

"What is that supposed to mean?" Her laugh was more sad than anything else.

"I mean that you need to get out of your head." Simon gestured around the room. "To get out of this house. You need some fresh air and some vitamin D."

Katrina laughed again, but this time it sounded more genuine. "Okay, Dr. Simon. What do you suggest?"

"How about we take a walk or go for a ride?"

She wrinkled her nose. "I spend enough time on those horses. But a walk sounds nice."

He got to his feet and held out his hand to her. She stared at it with surprise.

"Don't you want me to change into jeans first? Maybe sweats aren't the best choice."

He shrugged. "That's up to you. I would never dream of telling you to change into something else. I think you look good no matter what."

She smiled, and this time it reached her eyes, making them sparkle bluer than the sky. "You're sweet."

Simon jerked his chin toward the door. "How about we take that walk, then?"

Katrina looped her arm through his, and his heart leaped into his throat. From the age of sixteen, he'd had the biggest crush on this woman. She was everything he'd wanted for his future. She cared about her family, she was driven, and she was the smartest person he knew. If he were honest, he was secretly thrilled that she was back home. He'd missed her more than she would ever understand.

While he hated seeing her in pain over the loss of her job, he knew being home would do her good. The problem was that seeing her again only made his feelings for her intensify. And the way she would lean into him and tell all her deepest fears made him want to do everything in his power to make them go away.

He had to make sure not to let his feelings get the best of him. There was a certain distance he needed to maintain, and Brianne pushing Katrina to go on dates was just the thing to do it.

Except he hated it.

Already, he knew that watching her go on dates with the local guys would tear him up inside. None of the single, eligible men around here were good enough for her. They didn't understand that she needed more than just a ranch to run. Katrina needed to feel like she was the one in charge. And she needed everyone to know she was in control.

No one would be able to do that for her. Certainly not Jackson Duncan.

They exited the house and made it past the barn toward a trail that was frequented more by joggers than horse riders. The second the barn was out of view, Simon slowed his pace.

Katrina stopped and stared at him uncertainly. "What is it?"

"I have to tell you something. It's really important and I wanted to make sure we were completely alone."

Her eyes widened, searching his face. His heart hammered. The second he'd gotten off the phone with the lawyer, he knew he needed to call Katrina. But Brianne had called him first. She'd insisted they had to meet at the Reeses' ranch because she needed his help to convince their friend to finally go on that date before Jackson left.

There was only one problem. He wasn't sure what path he wanted to take, so he couldn't tell Brianne without first getting Katrina's advice.

Inhale.

Exhale.

He could do this.

Simon swallowed hard. "I know you're dealing with a lot right now, and it isn't fair to—"

She placed her hand on his forearm. "Whatever it is, I'm here for you. Just like you're here for me."

He nodded. "I know. It's just a lot to think about."

Katrina laughed softly. "Just tell me. It can't be as bad as what's been going on with me lately."

"So, you know how my grandfather had a small farm."

"Yeah," she drawled.

"But I was too young when he died, and they couldn't leave it to me."

"I know," she murmured.

They both knew how much he had wanted to keep his family's farm. It wasn't something his mother had wanted, which was why she'd moved to the city, and he'd made his peace with it. Only now, something had changed.

"Do you remember Mr. Granger? He owned a small farm on the other side of town. He was friends with my grandpa."

She nodded.

"Well, he passed away and… well… his lawyers just called me. They said he left me… *everything*."

Katrina gasped. "What?"

"I know. I don't believe it either. Apparently, he didn't have any children of his own. He'd been working that farm for ages and…" Simon shrugged. "I guess he wanted to give it to me."

"Why?" she blurted. "I mean, did he ever talk to you about it? I'm sorry, this just feels like it's coming clear out of left field."

"I know," he mumbled. "It is."

"What are you going to do?"

His eyes locked with hers. "Would it sound crazy if I wanted to keep it?"

WHEN YOU'RE FINALLY HOME

"What? Of course not."

"But I don't know anything about farming."

Katrina squeezed his arm where she'd still been holding him. "That's not true."

He laughed. "Yes, it is. I haven't helped out on a farm since I was a teenager. I don't know the first thing about running one. I'm a waiter at a restaurant, for Pete's sake."

"But it's in your blood. You could do it."

"That's just it. I'm not so sure I could."

Katrina gave him a flat look. "Don't sell yourself short. You know more about farming than..."

He pointed at her. "See? I don't have the faintest clue. What if I take it and I run it into the ground? I'm not an idiot. I know there are fees and taxes associated with it. If I can't afford to keep it running, then I'm going to have to sell anyway. Maybe it would be better if I just tell the lawyers that I can't take it. They'd probably help me find a buyer, right?"

She pressed her lips together in a firm line and stared hard at him.

"What?"

"Do you remember when we were kids and your grandfather's estate had to sell everything? There was barely enough left over to put into a trust for you. And the only thing you were worried about was that you wouldn't be able to do what your grandfather did. You wanted that farm more than anything."

"Yeah, well… I grew up. I know better now."

She snorted, causing his head to rear back. She placed her hands on either side of his face and her eyes bored into his. "This is your path. You can do it. Where is that optimistic person who helped me through some of the hardest moments and decisions of my life?"

"I guess that guy's just not sure if he can hack it. I'm not my most positive self right now."

"Well, I'm telling you that you can. And if you don't at least try, you're going to regret it for the rest of your life."

The corners of his lips quirked upward. "Okay, I think that's about the most honest thing you could have said to me."

She grinned, her smile widening. Then she slugged him in the shoulder before putting some distance between them. "Of course it is. And I can't wait to see what you make of it." Her eyes grew wide once more. "What does that mean for your job at the Lodge, I mean the Overlook Grand? You said you have to take a few extra shifts?"

He nodded. "I'm trying to save as much as I can so I have enough to get me by for the first little while. Then I'll put my two weeks' notice in as soon as the property is available."

Katrina let out a squeal of excitement. "I can't believe you didn't tell me sooner! This is amazing. It's everything you've ever wanted."

Well, not everything.

He glanced at her out of the corner of his eye as they continued down the path. He dredged up the courage to tell her the next step of his plan. "It's not going to be easy."

"No, I don't suppose it is. But you can handle it," she said confidently, tossing him her smile once more. It was the kind of smile that had his stomach in knots and his heart doing flips.

Simon took a deep breath and stopped walking again. "I'm going to need some help."

"What kind of help?"

"I don't know." He chuckled as he rubbed the back of his neck and looked away. "I don't suppose one of your brothers would be willing to help me get started. What do you think? Could I ask them?"

She cocked her head to the side and smiled broadly at him. "Of course my brothers would help. This is just the sort of thing they'd love to do."

"But I haven't been that close to them over the years. Our friendship was mostly just the two of us."

Her hand sliced through the air indifferently. "Bo is running the place more these days. Jack and Andrew just do what he tells them to do. And Daniel has tried to step up more. If I had to guess, I'd say Daniel would be the one you ask first. Maybe he'd even be willing to do a partnership of some kind."

"You really think so?"

"Sure. I'll even ask him with you." She made another excited noise. "I still can't believe it. Your dream is finally coming true." Then her features faltered.

Simon knew that look. She was thinking about her own shattered dreams. That look alone was proof she had no intentions of staying in Rocky Ridge as long as she had something to say about it. He'd just have to take advantage of every spare second he got with her.

CHAPTER THREE

Well, her life had just gotten worse.

Okay, that was harsh. Maybe a little on the dramatic side.

Katrina really was thrilled about Simon finding his happiness. She would never wish that this hadn't happened to him. He deserved it.

But there was a part of her that wished she had something, too.

Brianne and Simon were so happy. Their lives were coming together in a way that she could only dream would happen for herself. Brianne might not be dating anyone or have a huge career, but she was honest-to-goodness happy. And now Simon had a farm to run.

Where did that leave Katrina?

Feeling guilty because she was so dang jealous over what she didn't have. Why couldn't she find meaning in life without the career she wanted so badly? Why couldn't she just accept that her life was always meant to end up at

Rocky Ridge and she might as well give up on her dreams?

She sighed as she entered her bedroom, closing the door and leaning against it. Slowly, she dragged her body down it until she sat on the floor.

Everyone around her was right. She couldn't just stay locked in her room doing nothing. She had to get out there again and make something of herself. Submitting application after application was giving her zero results.

Katrina dug her fingers into her hair and closed her eyes tight. Her family wasn't as supportive as Simon had been. The way they looked at her with such disappointment only made matters worse.

Of course, it wasn't the same kind of disappointment as what she was experiencing. It was disappointment over the fact that she simply didn't feel like she belonged here.

Perhaps she needed to do something different—away from her family.

Maybe Simon would be willing to have her hang out at his farm while he got it ready for another season.

For the first time in weeks, Katrina felt a glimmer of hope. This wasn't the kind of hope that came with looking forward to a job offer. It was the kind that made her feel like everything would work out—eventually.

If she could get out from under the watchful gaze of her family and the pushiness of Brianne, then maybe she could find that light they were all telling her she needed to get back.

WHEN YOU'RE FINALLY HOME

∽

"If you're going to be here, you might as well grab a shovel and help me muck these stalls." Simon held out the offensive object toward her and Katrina smirked.

"You realize that my hiding out here was meant to be an escape from the work my brothers were trying to make me do."

It had been a whole month since he'd found out about the farm, and he'd finally gotten all the paperwork in order.

Simon gestured with the shovel again, drawing her attention to it.

"You have to be kidding."

"If you're going to be here while I'm working, you get to help. Simple as that."

She rolled her eyes and took the shovel. "Fine, but I'm not going to be happy about it."

He didn't even seem to try to hide his smile, and that fact alone brought a grin to her own face.

Katrina moved into the stall beside him. "So, what's your plan? Are you going to keep this place operating like Mr. Granger had it going?"

"I don't even know what that means," Simon shot a look over the side of the stall before he lunged forward and scooped up the old hay from the previous residents.

"What I mean is that Mr. Granger clearly used this as a dairy farm. He had a whole herd of cows and some goats and chickens. But mostly cows."

"Yeah, I'm aware."

Katrina placed a hand on her hip. "Or you could use the land to grow crops that the other ranchers need. Or—"

"Okay, okay, I get it," Simon murmured. "I guess I never really thought about it."

She lifted a brow. "Really? You've known about this for the last month, and you haven't decided how you want to run it?"

"What do you expect?" He smirked at her. "I'm not the planner you are. I'm just trying to keep my head above water. There's a lot to do. I didn't realize how much I'd need to get done before I can bring Maisy and Jewel from where they're being boarded."

Katrina paused. "I didn't realize you still had your grandpa's horses."

A soft smile touched his lips even as he continued working. "Of course I do. They were too young to do anything with when we were teens, but I've been working with them a lot lately and I can't wait for them to come here. I bet they'll love the pastures—all that space to run around."

"I'm sure you're right."

They continued working in silence for a few minutes before she stopped again. "How is everything going now that the estate is settled?"

This time, Simon slowed his work as he glanced at her sideways. "I really am in over my head."

"Well, what did Daniel say? You called him, right?" Based on the chagrined look on his face, she had her answer.

"Simon! I told you to talk to him. He's gonna be your best shot at getting this place where you want it to be."

"I know. But it's like you said. If I don't know what I'm going to do with this place, then what good will his help be? I need a plan, right?"

Her hands on her hips, she stood there probably looking more like an unhappy parent than his friend. Slowly, she dropped her arms. "Yeah. I guess you're right. So let's figure that out."

"You don't have to help with that."

"Sure I do. When I needed someone to help me get out of my funk, you were there. Tell me what your passions are."

He shot her a funny look then laughed. "I don't think—"

"*Don't* think. Just blurt out the first thing that comes to your mind. What kind of place do you want to run? Where do you see yourself in five years?"

"Training horses," he blurted. His eyes widened and his brows shot up.

Her expression mirrored his. "Really?"

He put the shovel down and leaned it against the wall. "Yeah. I guess so."

"Where did that come from?"

Simon shrugged. "I don't know. I don't even have that much experience with horses besides Maisy and Jewel. I don't know if I'd be any good at it."

She worried her lower lip.

"What?" he demanded. "I know that look. You're not sure about something."

"Yeah..." she hedged. "I'm not."

"Well, what is it?" He moved closer, crossing his arms on the edge of the half-wall that separated them. "I need to know. You're the one I trust the most. You're my closest friend."

Katrina's eyes flitted to meet his. "It's just that... Well, I think that might be something that takes a lot of time. You need to develop a good base of customers—surrounding ranchers who need your kind of expertise. And you don't really have expertise to sell. You would need to get some training yourself or at least offer some training free of charge to get some reviews. It's going to take a lot of work—"

"You asked what my passion was. Not what was the down-to-earth idea," he mumbled.

This was the first time she'd seen him not over-the-moon optimistic. In fact, he looked completely mortified over what he'd just admitted.

She charged forward and placed her hand on his arm. "Hey, you're right. I did ask about your passion, and it's not impossible."

"Really? Because you're definitely making it sound like it's something I can't do."

Katrina offered him a wan smile. It was the best she could do in light of the current circumstances. What had he expected? She was the logical one of the bunch. If he'd wanted someone to be his cheerleader, he should have told Brianne.

"You know me. I'm going to look at things in a different way. But when I say that I know it's possible, then you should take that for what it is."

"Okay, so if you think it's possible, what would you do if you were in my situation?"

She pressed her lips together and her eyes narrowed. There were several things she might do to start with. But most of them took money—money that Simon didn't have. He would have to get a loan and she was fairly certain he didn't want to sink any more money into this than he already had.

"I guess I would start with what you have. You need a cashflow that will allow you to invest in your future."

He nodded. "That makes a lot of sense."

Katrina gestured toward the door. "Mr. Gregory used this as a dairy farm. It wasn't the biggest in the area, but it did provide quality milk and there will still be a market for it. We could ask around to find out who his customers were then see if they'd like to continue with you. Of course, that would mean getting some cows."

That was when Simon's grin widened. "They weren't able to find a buyer. The lawyer said that they were tasked with finding a buyer within the first forty-five days and if they couldn't, the cows would revert to me."

Katrina gasped. "Well, you should have led with that. Way to bury the lede! Why didn't you say something sooner?"

He shrugged. "Because I really don't like cows."

She laughed. It was nice to have a reason to laugh lately, and being with Simon seemed to do that for her. There was something about being around him that relieved her of the pressure to be happy. Simon didn't care if she was down in the dumps. He didn't treat her any differently. And at the same time, he could say things or give her looks that put her at ease.

"Okay, so it's settled. We'll do the dairy farm until we can get the horse training project underway."

"We?" He eyed her. "Are you sure you want to get those pretty boots of your dirty?"

Katrina lifted her rubber boots and wrinkled her nose. "These ones?"

He chuckled. "You're not going to be able to help with the cows in those. I'm talking about the cowboy boots you wear at your place. You seem to forget that I've seen them. They're still brand-spanking new and they're just for looks."

She snorted. "Yours are new, too."

"I have an excuse," he shot back. "This farm is brand new, and along with everything else, I have to break it in."

"Fair enough. And no, I'm not worried about my boots. I'd rather be here with the cows who are less temperamental than the animals who roam around our place."

"How do you know they're less temperamental?"

The look she gave him was completely serious, but it took everything she had in her to utter the next words with a straight face. "Have you *met* my brothers?"

For a moment, he didn't seem to understand her joke. But before she could lay it out for him, he let out a dry laugh. "Ah, I see what you did there. Your brothers are the animals."

Katrina tapped the tip of her nose. "See? I can be funny, too."

"Ha… ha," he mumbled. "Very funny. I really hope you don't talk about me like that."

"What? Of course not. You're my closest friend. I would never dream of comparing you to my brothers." She gave him a wicked grin. "But an animal? I make no promises."

He rolled his eyes. "How about you get back to work. We still have a lot to do and now that I know what I'm going to do with those cattle, I'll have to call the company that's been caring for them and have them get delivered. You sure your brother will help out with that side of things?"

"I know he will. Daniel's gonna flip over being asked."

Once again, they fell into comfortable silence. This was nice. There weren't many people she could do this with— just being herself. She could quietly despair over the state of her life, while every so often being there for one of her best friends. Simon deserved every bit of happiness and if he wanted to train horses, then she was going to make sure that happened before she found her job. With all the resumés she'd submitted, she should probably call in a few favors to the folks who were friends with her parents so she wasn't hired before she could ensure Simon's success.

There might not be a lot of people who would want to help her specifically, but her last name still carried some weight. And she'd gotten to know the Holt triplets up on the hill a little bit more since they'd moved to the area. If anyone could spread the news about what Simon wanted to do, it would be Kelsey. She had her fingers on every social media platform.

Hopefully, she'd be willing to help Simon out.

CHAPTER FOUR

Day after miserable day, Simon was reminded just how deep in the zone he'd been pushed. He couldn't think of a single moment when Katrina didn't make it perfectly clear where they stood.

He was in the zone, alright.

The *friend* zone.

And he hated it—which was utterly ridiculous.

Simon didn't want to be a love interest when it came to Katrina. If he was, he'd only get his heart broken. So why couldn't he just brush it off whenever she said he was her dearest friend?

Because it rubbed him the wrong way. But it shouldn't. Being her friend was important, but being in the friend zone was different.

What if he changed his mind? What if he wanted to fight for her? The guys Brianne had lined up for Katrina to go out with had nothing on him. He'd never try to get Katrina do anything that didn't make her happy. He'd be all in to help her reach any goal she wanted to reach. And that could be a problem if she didn't want to stay in town.

Simon knocked on the door at the Reese family house then moved to the side and leaned his back against the wood siding. What was he thinking? He was smarter than this. There was far too much to worry about with his own future and he needed to focus on that. The last thing he needed to worry about was Katrina's dating life. She'd already gone on four dates with three guys and each time he saw her afterwards, he held his breath.

While he knew the chances of her finding someone were slim, he couldn't help but worry that she might just click with someone.

And each time he saw her and all she could do was talk about how the guy wasn't her type, his blood pressure returned to normal. He wasn't sure how many more of these dates he would be able to handle. Brianne was doing too good of a job finding guys that Katrina had never met before and all he wanted to do was pull her aside and tell her to take it easy.

Simon glanced at the door, his brows furrowed. Katrina had told him to stop by this afternoon so she could tell him something. He was here on time. Where was she?

He turned to knock again, but before his fist made contact with the door, it swung inward.

"See? I told you. Simon and I are going out tonight," Katrina called into the house. She poked her head outside and winked at him. "I'll tell you later." Then she called again, "No, it's not what you think. We're just friends."

A muffled sound was all he heard when the person she'd been yelling to called back.

Katrina rolled her eyes. "It's not gonna happen, Mom." This time, her voice lowered several decibels and the irritation returned. This was the Katrina he was more familiar with. She was still struggling to find a job that she wanted, and while she seemed to perk up a little when he was able to get her out of the house, it wasn't much.

Her mother's faint voice grew a little louder, but before Simon could figure out what she was saying, Katrina slammed the door shut. She grabbed Simon's hand and yanked him forward.

"Hurry! She's coming."

"Wha—"

"I'll tell you in the car."

"But I wasn't expecting—"

"Don't worry, if you're busy, you can just drop me off in town somewhere. I need to get out of the house." She was breathless by the time they made it to his car. Her hand released his the second before she opened the door and launched herself inside.

Simon spared one brief second to glance back at the house, finding Jennifer Reese on the porch, staring at them with a funny little grin on her face. He offered her a wave and she waved back.

Katrina laid on the horn and he jumped before hurrying around to the other side and getting in. His friend shot him a death glare. "What are you doing?"

"I was waving to your mother."

"You mean you were fraternizing with the enemy."

"The enemy?" He laughed. "What happened today?"

Katrina motioned toward the ignition. "I'm not saying a word until you get me out of here."

"As you wish." Simon pushed the key into the ignition and turned it. "But I can't just hang out today. I have to go to the used car lot. Jeff said he had a truck that just came in and I might be able to get it for a good enough price that my monthly payment will be next to nothing."

Katrina wrinkled her nose. "You can't trust Jeff."

"What? Why?"

She gave him a hard stare. "Have you ever gotten a truck from him?"

"Well… no. You've seen the cars I've driven over the years."

"Then trust me. You need to go to Billings to get the best price on something. There are more lots out there and some of the salesmen are *really* pushy, but if you don't let them jerk you around, then you'll end up with something you won't regret five hundred miles down the road."

Simon shot a look at her out of the corner of his eye. "That sounds like the words of boring Katrina."

She sucked in and swung around to stare at him. He couldn't see her eyes, but he could feel them drilling into him like they were laser beams. "*What*? Did you just call me boring?"

WHEN YOU'RE FINALLY HOME

He bit back a smile.

"Simon, do you really want to be locked into a truck that's going to bleed you dry? Trust me. I have four brothers. And every single time they have gotten a truck, it was at this one place in Billings. I swear, if you don't go there, you're going to regret it."

"Now you just sound threatening."

"Good. So maybe now you'll listen to what I have to say."

He chuckled despite himself. "Okay, then Billings it is. I bet there will be a few places open by the time we get there."

She settled back in her seat. "Sounds perfect to me."

"Are you going to tell me what was going on back there?" Simon relaxed a little, too. For the next couple of hours, he had Katrina all to himself. He didn't have to worry about her going out on a date with anyone else, and the cherry on top was that he'd be able to get her advice on something he wasn't one hundred percent confident he could do.

Katrina sighed and the light shining from her face faded. "My mom has gotten it into her head that since I'm letting Brianne set me up on dates, she gets to do it too."

"Uh-oh."

"Uh-oh is right. First of all, no. I do not want to date the son of the woman she met at the grocery store. I don't want to date the nephew of the woman from her book club. And I definitely don't want to meet the kid who I vaguely remember sticking gum in my hair when we were in preschool."

Simon chuckled.

"It's not funny! This is getting ridiculous. Just because I'm letting my friend get me out there doesn't mean I've been enjoying it. A relationship is *not* a top priority. Besides, I'm only doing it for Brianne because she lives vicariously through me."

"Are you sure?"

She shifted in her seat and her voice thinned. "I don't know what you're talking about."

"Are you sure," he drawled, "that you don't want to change your priorities around just a little? This is your future we're talking about. You just might meet your soulmate."

He'd meant it in a teasing way, but by the way the car got quiet, he instantly regretted his statement.

"I guess you make a good point."

"Really?"

"*No!* When have I ever wanted to date someone over doing something that pertained to my career? I thought you knew me better than that."

He breathed out a silent sigh of relief for no other reason than he wasn't prepared to watch her fall for someone that wasn't him. If there was even a chance that she would stay in Rocky Ridge for a guy, he would want to be considered. Thankfully, that didn't seem to be something that would happen any time soon.

Simon stole a glance at her and turned his focus to the road. "So, you used me as an excuse."

"You mad?" She didn't even try to lie about it.

He shook his head. "We're always going to be there for each other, right?"

She nodded. "Yeah."

That was it, then. She trusted him. The only reason she'd called him was so he could rescue her from her meddling family.

The remainder of the drive passed in silence. She didn't even look at her phone the whole way there. Then again, he wasn't sure she hadn't left it behind. The companionable silence was something he'd grown used to, though he couldn't deny how nice it would have been to have her chatting about something. He loved the sound of her voice more than the country music stations she picked out.

When they got into town, she directed him to a used car lot where she assured him he'd get the best bang for his buck. He pulled into the parking lot and they both got out. Katrina gestured out at the sea of cars and trucks then beamed at him.

"See what I'm talking about? This is perfect. So many options to choose from."

Just then, another car pulled in behind them. Simon squinted and his stomach dropped. It was Brianne. He glanced with confusion at Katrina.

She let out a laugh. "I told Brianne to meet us here so we could do something fun afterward. I feel like we're not spending nearly enough time together since she started setting me up on those dates and I've been hanging with you in my spare time."

"Yeah, that's a great idea," he lied. Car shopping with Katrina was one thing. But to have Brianne tag along made it not so great.

He refused to admit that he'd been hoping this was sort of like the date they'd never had before. Because he wasn't going to let his heart get broken.

Even still, he hated seeing her run across the lot to the other car and throw her arms around their friend. Heaving a disappointed sigh, Simon strode toward the small metal building on the far side of the property. All he had to do was get a truck that could tow a trailer. Nothing with bells and whistles.

By the time he had listed all the details of what he wanted to the salesman, Brianne and Katrina had made it to his side.

The salesman eyed the two women and winked at Simon. "Lucky you."

Brianne and Katrina looked at each other and released the most embarrassingly loud laugh. "We're not with him." Brianne continued laughing. "We're just friends."

That was when Simon saw the amused sort of pity in the guy's eyes. For a reason Simon didn't quite understand, a flurry of frustration flooded his insides. He shoved his hands into his pockets and stared pointedly at the salesman. "Is there anything you have on this lot that fits my requirements?"

"Right. Of course, young man. Follow me." The man led the way, followed by Simon and finally the two women, who were laughing and talking quietly. It wasn't helping his case one iota. If he'd been here with Katrina all on her own, he might have been able to make it seem like they were together and he was a calm, capable individual who knew what he wanted and how to get it.

As it stood, he was having a hard time not reading into every look this guy was shooting in their direction.

"We've been friends since grade school. We're just meeting up for dinner. You know, to catch up," Simon clarified. He didn't know if the guy would respond or if he would even care at this point. For now, Simon just wanted the salesman to stop gawking at him like he was the guy's next mark.

They stopped by a white Ford that was covered in rust.

Brianne scrunched up her face and looked toward Simon with disdain. "You're not gonna get this, are you? It looks like it belongs in a junk yard."

Simon shot a wary eye toward the salesman, who seemed to also be curious whether Simon would close the deal. Great. If he thought Simon could be swayed, he might take all three of them to something newer. The price on the truck was reasonable as long as it had everything Simon needed. He just wished the girls would walk away so he could have the discussion in private.

He shot them a look he prayed they'd understand. Brianne's expression was blank, but Katrina came to the rescue.

"Hey, Brianne, let's go look at those coupes." She wheeled her friend away and for the second time that day, she winked at Simon.

"Yeah, sure there's nothing going on." The sales guy nudged Simon briefly. "I can see it. There's absolutely something there."

"Lucky for me, I didn't come here to talk about my love life. So how about you give me the information you have on this truck."

CHAPTER FIVE

Katrina sat beside Brianne and across from Simon at the restaurant that the former had suggested. Already, she could tell Simon wasn't as happy as he'd been when he'd picked her up. It was minor, but she could sense that he was dealing with some frustration.

She wasn't sure why, however, because he'd ended up with the truck he'd wanted.

A truck, by the way, that Brianne thought was far too rusted to possibly run well.

Simon stared hard at his menu, not looking up at either of them. Brianne was talking at hyper speed, her voice an octave above where it normally was. Unfortunately, Katrina couldn't focus on what her friend was saying when Simon seemed to be in a foul mood. This wasn't normal. Something must have happened.

"Simon," she leaned over the table and whispered, "what's going on?"

Brianne's boisterous chatter subsided and her eyes turned toward Simon, who glanced up briefly and shook his head.

"Nothing."

"You look upset."

"Well, I'm not." He flashed her a smile, but it wasn't one she was used to. It didn't reach his eyes, for one. And there was a tension at the corners like he was being controlled by a puppeteer.

"I can tell—"

He set his eyes on Brianne. "So, who's next on your list of suitors?"

Brianne laughed. "Really? That's what you want to talk about? I thought you hated when I brought up anything to do with those guys."

"Well, it's better than hearing you talk about the out-of-towners who have been visiting your mother's jewelry shop."

Still, Simon's smile didn't seem quite right. Katrina couldn't put a finger on just what was off about it, though, and she knew better than to ask.

Brianne glanced toward Katrina. "I know you said you weren't interested in going out with Jackson Duncan again… but—"

Katrina held up both hands, her mood completely destroyed. "No. I'm not interested. I told you. I'm not going to see him again."

Brianne pouted. "But *why*? He said you were really interesting and even though he's doesn't live close to town, he's willing to drive all the way here to see you again."

Katrina shook her head.

"What if I told you that he can't stop thinking about you?"

She peeked at her friend but didn't agree to anything right away.

"See? I knew you would perk up. And on top of that, he lives just outside of Billings. If things worked out between you two, then you could be married to a cowboy *and* have your dream job there. Doesn't that sound amazing?"

"For the love of all that is holy, Brianne. Will you stop pushing her to do something she doesn't want to do?"

Both Katrina and Brianne turned surprised eyes on Simon. She'd never heard his voice so heavy and sharp at the same time. His attitude was finally shining through in an undeniable way.

"What?" Brianne laughed, but it was strained. "Are you upset that Katrina is dating again?"

His eyes rounded, then flitted to Katrina and back to Brianne. "Of course not."

"Then why are you suddenly so vocal about who she sees?"

Once again, there was some hesitation. If Katrina was even a degree more confident in what she was reading, she might have assumed that Simon's displeasure came from a slight jealousy.

But that was ridiculous. He wasn't jealous of the guys she was dating—going on dates with. He was just protective. After all that talk she'd given him on the way to the city about not wanting her mother to pressure her into seeing certain guys, he was probably just coming to her rescue when he noticed that Brianne was attempting to steamroll her.

"Simon, don't worry about it," Katrina hedged. "Brianne is just trying to help." She glanced over to her friend, who still didn't seem all that happy with Simon's sharp tone.

"Yeah," Brianne muttered. "If Katrina didn't want to go, she would have said something."

"She *did* say something," Simon insisted.

Then, all at once, the dynamic changed. Brianne flashed a wide smile. "I think someone's crushing on Katrina," she said in a sing-song voice.

Simon flushed all the way up to his ears. "You'd better not be talking about me. I have zero interest in dating someone who could have been my sister in another life."

Even as he said it, something inside of her shifted. Not once had he compared her to being his sibling in all the years they were friends. She hadn't realized it until this moment.

And now that she'd heard it from his lips, she couldn't deny just how strange it felt. She'd never thought of him as anything more than a friend, but there must have been some part of her deep down that had wanted the possibility of something more to occur.

Because now her stomach swirled with regret and disappointment.

What was happening to her? She wasn't supposed to want to be with Simon in *that* way.

Brianne gave a triumphant smile. "Well, then. That settles it. If you don't want to date her, then you must hate Jackson."

"That guy would be a terrible fit for her and we all know it."

Brianne leaned forward, her eyes flashing. Katrina had never seen them so at odds with one another. It was almost like they were now competing for the same gig. Did Simon want a turn at setting her up?

That thought was almost laughable.

Almost.

There was a slight pique of curiosity that fluttered through Katrina's body. What kind of guy would he pick to set her up with?

Katrina placed her hand on the table between the two of them if only to get their attention on her again. "If you don't want me to go on a second date with Jackson, then who would you suggest?"

Surprise seemed to slap both of her friends in the face. They turned to face her then looked at each other again. Brianne's expression was the first to shift into something more victorious than anything else.

"See? You can't think of someone who would be better than Jackson."

Simon worked his jaw for a moment before he settled back in his seat and crossed his arms. "I think we could do better than Jackson Duncan. But if you're so interested, Katrina, go for it. See what a second date would do."

That wasn't the reaction she'd expected from him. She almost wished he would tell her that he wanted to take her out and show her what a real man could be. But then again, that was the kind of stuff fairytales were made of—and this was most definitely not a fairytale.

Simon wasn't her Prince Charming in disguise. And Brianne wasn't a fairy godmother.

Katrina would have told Brianne no, even with the added information that Jackson hadn't been able to stop thinking about her. But with Simon egging her on, she didn't really have any other choice. She needed to prove to him that she was willing to take chances, too.

Ironic, seeing as Simon hadn't ever been the friend who pushed her to do things. That was Brianne's territory. If anything, Simon was the one who told her to find joy wherever she could get it. And that might be what she was about to do.

Katrina lifted her chin and set a firm gaze on her other friend. "Fine. Tell him that I'll go out with him again. And make sure he comes to pick me up, because I'm not going to meet him this time."

She could have sworn that Simon's gaze darkened ever so slightly. However, when she looked closer, he'd put on a mask again. It wasn't a literal one, but the way his eyes seemed to cloud over and his muscles relaxed, she couldn't get a read on him.

Oh well.

Brianne, on the other hand was ecstatic. She threw her arms around Katrina's shoulders. "This is the one. I can feel it. You guys just didn't click right away. And besides, it's not like love at first sight is real. You have to get to know someone before you can say for certain if they're the one." She squealed again. "I can't wait."

"Sheesh, if you like him so much, maybe you should date him," Simon muttered.

Brianne laughed, placing her elbow on the table so she could put her chin in her hand. "You know, I could probably find someone for you, too. You just have to tell me what you like." She gave Katrina a pointed look. "Have you ever paid attention to who Simon is interested in? It's been forever since he went on a date. Unless he's just not telling us?"

Katrina glanced at Simon. Brianne was right. Simon's love life was more of a secret than anything else in their little group. It made sense, though. He was a guy. Talking about girls he liked with his friends who were also girls probably spelled trouble. Brianne wasn't against telling him exactly what she thought of some of the women who grew up in Rocky Ridge.

Simon avoided looking directly at her. At least, that was how it felt, but she might just be internalizing everything. He was upset with her for some reason, so it was easy to assume he was closing himself off from her.

"Let's just leave him alone, okay, Brianne?"

Her friend shot her a funny look before glancing toward Simon. She studied him for a moment and nodded almost imperceptibly. The rest of their meal was eaten while chatting about anything that didn't have to do with relationships or dating. Katrina continued to sneak glances at Simon and resolved to have a private conversation with him when they were alone.

Unfortunately, that didn't seem likely today.

Brianne grabbed onto Katrina's arm as soon as they left the restaurant. "Shopping spree."

Katrina shot another look in Simon's direction, pleading with him to come up with an excuse, but he wasn't paying attention. "I don't think I have time—"

"Nonsense. We're all the way out here already. You might as well come to a few shops." Brianne tugged on her again and Katrina glanced at Simon, who was staring at his phone.

"I came with Simon—"

"Simon doesn't mind, do you?" Brianne tugged on Katrina again. "And he's more than welcome to come with."

This time he looked up, one brow lifting. "Pass."

Brianne laughed. "I figured. You've never been interested in coming with us when we go shopping."

"Are you sure you don't want company for the ride home?" Katrina tried to hint, but Simon had become utterly clueless.

He shook his head. "I need to get back and do a few things before they deliver the cows on Monday." He didn't meet her eyes. He continued to stare at his phone until, with one fleeting glance in her general direction, he offered them both a small wave.

"Cows? What's that about?" Brianne asked.

Katrina gasped. "That's right. He hasn't told you yet."

"Hasn't told me what?"

"He inherited the dairy farm that Mr. Gregory ran."

Brianne's eyes rounded bigger than saucers. She whacked at Katrina playfully. "Why didn't you guys say something? That's so exciting for him. Hasn't he said he always felt like he should be in charge of a farm or something?"

"Actually, he wants to turn it into a horse training business."

"Wow," Brianne murmured as she glanced in the direction where Simon had gone. "That's a lot."

"I know. But he thinks he can do it." Katrina sent one more fleeting look toward Simon. "And I think he'll be able to do it, too. He just needs a little bit of help. He's gonna ask Daniel for some tips."

"Well, that's cool for him." Brianne's focus shifted once again to Katrina. "Now, let's see about finding you something hot."

Katrina rolled her eyes. "There isn't a place in town I think Jackson would take me to where I don't have something to fit the mood."

Brianne shook her head resolutely. "You need to feel beautiful, too."

She scoffed. "And you think my wardrobe doesn't make me feel beautiful? I feel beautiful."

Her friend wrinkled her nose and they both laughed. "But seriously, you can't go on a date with him in old jeans and you definitely can't go in a pantsuit. So let's find you a dress." Brianne gasped. "I know the perfect place."

CHAPTER SIX

Three days since Katrina had been on a date with Jackson Duncan.

Three whole days and Simon hadn't seen her or heard an update.

This was bad. It was *really* bad.

Katrina had asked him if she should go on a second date with the guy and he'd been stupid enough to tell her yes. Heck, he'd all but pushed her off the cliff to a waiting cowboy who had everything going for him.

Simon seethed, hating the way his own choices had put him in this situation. Now he was distracted. He didn't know what he was doing with the dairy farm. Every day, a new roadblock would materialize, and he found himself wishing he had just sold the farm to the highest bidder.

What was it about this town that made him feel like he deserved to be part of any of it?

He had no family. He was an orphan with nothing and no one. He'd lost everyone.

Okay, that was disingenuous.

The Reese family had taken him in when he really didn't have anyone. They'd been the family he needed when he'd hit rock bottom. Jennifer had taken him under her wing and helped him see there was still good in the world.

She was the one he had to thank for his optimistic outlook.

And all it had taken was one person to tear all that optimism away from him. He didn't blame Brianne. It was like Katrina had pointed out, she was just trying to help. Katrina had hit a new low and she needed something to look forward to.

But why did it have to be a *guy*?

The cow beside him mooed so loudly that Simon jumped. He took a step to the side and gawked at the animal. He'd had the animals for just over a week and he'd never heard one quite so obnoxious.

"What do you want? You've been fed. You've been milked."

The cow shook her head like a wet dog might have done. It was about time to send his small herd out to a pasture to get some sun and exercise anyway. That was something he could do without the help of others.

He still hadn't reached out to Daniel. Simon wanted to make sure he did everything that he could handle on his own before seeking out additional help. That way, he'd get the most out of that assistance.

His reasons went beyond that mentality. He also didn't want to make himself look like he couldn't handle being a farmer. Daniel was Katrina's brother and as such, he figured there would be conversations about him between them.

At least that was what he assumed happened between siblings.

Simon got the cattle out of the milking machines he'd finally figured out how to operate and let them wander freely. It had taken a lot longer to do that chore than he would have thought and once he was done, he checked his phone.

Still no word from Katrina. She'd said she didn't want to hang around her family's ranch lately because she couldn't stand her family trying to make her feel better about her lack of job prospects. So why hadn't she stopped by yesterday? She'd been here every Monday through Friday since he'd been handed the key.

Something told him he already knew the answer, though he refused to admit it.

Katrina had actually hit it off with that Duncan guy.

Simon had lost his opportunity to be with her, and nothing made that realization more real than not hearing from her.

His frustrations continued to mount until all he wanted to do was storm over to her place and tell her all the reasons she didn't have to lower her standards. She wanted to be in the city, right? She deserved to be happy.

And if she was so willing to settle for country life, then why not choose him?

His chest was tight, unyielding in the constrictions of his lungs and heart. While he was still breathing normally, he didn't feel like he was getting nearly enough oxygen. Simon clutched at his shirt and tugged at it as if that alone would help alleviate the symptoms he was experiencing.

He spent the rest of the day throwing himself into his work until he couldn't take the silence anymore. He needed to see her, to ask her how it went if only for his own sanity.

When Simon arrived at her place, the sun had already begun to sink behind the tree line. The property was cast in a golden hue from the brilliant sky overhead. Normally, he would have allowed himself a moment to reflect and appreciate the way it shined.

But not today.

He'd been helping Katrina deal with the loss of her job and the heartache that had caused for too long to let her just brush him off when something better came along. He might not be dating material, but he was still her friend and she needed to accept it.

Simon hurried up the steps to the house and rapped his knuckles against the mahogany-stained wood. The sound echoed through the air, reverberating against the structures and trees in the vicinity. He turned away from the door to gaze out at the beauty of the Reese ranch. This place was the reason he wanted to stay in Rocky Ridge even when all of his family was gone.

This place made him realize he was home.

The door behind him swung open and he braced himself to let Katrina have it, but Jennifer's voice caught him before he made a complete fool of himself.

"Simon? How are you doing?"

He faced her and offered her a surprised smile. "I was just coming by to see if Katrina was doing okay. She was planning on stopping by my farm today."

Her face brightened. "That's right! She told me that Mr. Gregory left you his farm. That's so exciting. How is it going?"

"There's a definite learning curve... but Katrina...?"

"Right! She went out for a ride. I can tell her you stopped by—"

Simon cut her off. "I'll wait for her in the barn if that's okay. I'm sure she won't be out much later. She doesn't like riding in the dark."

Jennifer smiled. She was as close to a mother as he had these days and just knowing she was here seemed to calm his worried heart. "Of course. You know where it is."

He nodded, waved, and hurried down the steps toward the barn. Simon found himself a bench to sit on and waited. He tapped his fingers on his knees and glanced at the clock several times in the span of ten minutes before he finally heard the sound of approaching hoofbeats.

Simon jumped to his feet the second Katrina entered the barn. She pulled up on the reins and stared at him with surprise. "Simon? What are you doing here?"

He fought the instinct to get upset with her question. Had she forgotten so quickly that she was supposed to be helping him? What had happened to their plans? His jaw tightened as he moved to her side and helped her from the saddle. It was more out of habit than anything else, but somehow it felt different when he lowered her to her feet.

His hands lingered at her waist, as did hers at his shoulders. Simon's eyes locked with Katrina's and for the briefest of moments, he could believe she had feelings for him. If his heart hadn't already been running a thousand miles a minute, it would have started.

Katrina was the first to move. She blinked and pulled her hands from his shoulders, but due to the horse behind her, she couldn't step back. Simon dropped his hands to his sides and cleared his throat. He had to remember why he came here in the first place.

"You didn't come to my farm yesterday."

Her eyes widened. "Oh my gosh, I totally forgot to call you. We had some animals get out and I had to help bring them back. It was... a lot." Her voice drifted toward the end of her statement, growing softer. "Is that why you came? To ask me why I wasn't there?"

"You didn't come today, either."

She dropped her focus to her feet. "Brianne insisted on having a girls' day after we went shopping last weekend. I could have sworn I messaged you, but maybe I forgot to press send."

"Really? You expect me to believe that?" Simon shook his head and swallowed back the irritation that continued to grow. "You've never forgotten to let me know before. It's like you've suddenly forgotten about me."

Her eyes cut to meet his. "That's not true," she insisted. "There's just a lot going on right now. First, the date went terrible—"

"It did?" Simon almost hated how hopeful his voice. He cleared his throat again and lowered the tone in an attempt to cover it up. "What happened?"

She shrugged. "I don't want to get into it. Let's just say that he thought that I should let go of my dream job." Katrina's deep breath shook slightly even as she exhaled. "I think Brianne felt partially responsible and wanted to make me feel better."

"He's an idiot," Simon muttered, drawing Katrina's attention again. "If a guy can't see that something makes you happy, then he's not worth it. You deserve better."

This was the closest he'd ever come to telling her his true feelings. He wanted to tell her that he thought she was amazing, that she could do whatever she had her heart set on. But something held him back.

Words were cheap, anyway. He'd said those things before in different ways over the years and they'd never quite had the impact he'd wanted them to. At this point, he might have better luck showing her that he wanted to toss his hat into the ring.

Simon inched closer, studying her eyes as he did. She didn't shy away from him; if anything, she stood her ground more firmly. Katrina lifted her chin and her lips parted just slightly. She exhaled, and his heart thrummed with the anticipation of what he was about to do.

One kiss.

One kiss was all it would take to change their lives forever. This could go either way. They were standing on a tightrope, swaying one way and then the next. For all he knew, this kiss could destroy the friendship they'd built, though he felt that was more improbable than simply being embarrassed that they'd tried.

What if this kiss was all it took for them to realize what they'd been putting off for so long? He could sense it—the electricity, the anticipation. Everything hung on this moment.

And it all came crashing to a halt.

"Wow! Did you see that lightning storm in the distance?" Brianne's call was followed by the sound of hooves approaching. Simon and Katrina flung apart as if lightning itself had struck the ground between them just as Brianne entered the barn leading a saddled mare.

How had he not seen her car? Was it even out there? He clung to the wall of the barn, watching as she strode straight toward Katrina.

"Geez, you ride fast. I thought you would have already taken off the saddle by now." Brianne pulled her hat from her head and ran a hand through her pink hair. Simon's presence caught her eye then because she glanced toward him and smiled broadly. "Hey, Simon! Why are you here? Are you finally asking Daniel for help? Katrina said you needed some." She put her hat back on her head and placed her hand on her hip. "I'm still mad at you, by the way. How come you didn't tell me about the farm?"

Simon pursed his lips, exhaling out his nose and pushed away from the wall. "Because you don't care much about farming." It was the only thing he could think of to say.

She huffed. "I'm your friend, too. You can tell me stuff like this. Just because I don't do the ranching thing for a job doesn't mean I wouldn't care." She handed Katrina the reins for her horse and hurried toward him.

He stiffened when she threw her arms around his neck. His eyes drifted to Katrina, locking on her. Those few seconds stretched on for an eternity. Simon would have given anything just to hear her thoughts. Was she relieved? Disappointed? What would she have done if they weren't interrupted?

All too quickly, Brianne pulled back. "I think we need to have a housewarming party. We can invite as many people as you want. And if you're lucky, people will get you stuff you actually need." She frowned, tapping her chin. "What *do* you need?"

Behind her, Katrina chuckled. She took the reins of both horses while Brianne drilled him with questions, most of which he had no answers for. Every so often, he'd catch Katrina watching him and his heart would start its dance all over again.

CHAPTER SEVEN

The next few days, Katrina made sure she was up as early as her brothers so she could get what few things they needed help with done. That way, she was ready to head over to Simon's farm by the time the sun was fully risen.

They hadn't talked about what had nearly happened in the barn on Tuesday. And the longer she waited for him to bring it up, the more she started to wonder if she'd imagined the whole thing.

Every so often, she'd catch him glancing in her direction, to which she'd just smile and ask him a question about whatever he was working on. She'd never thought that farming equipment could be so interesting.

Okay, it really wasn't. But there was something about being around Simon. Even if he was only telling her what he'd been learning about on the internet, she enjoyed simply spending time with him. He'd already figured out how to change spark plugs for the tractor, how to troubleshoot the milking machine for the two dozen cows he was now raising, and he was getting involved in anything he could to learn as much as he could.

When Katrina wasn't at his farm, she was thinking about what they'd talk about when they saw each other again. Those nagging doubts and worries about her future with interior design had faded, allowing her to prioritize the deepening friendships she had with those she'd grown up with.

Throughout the week, Katrina spent most of her time with Simon, coming up with excuses whenever anyone asked where she was going. On the weekends, she'd hang out with Brianne.

Since Simon hadn't been willing to bring up their near-kiss, Katrina had continued to allow Brianne to set her up with various guys—something that still seemed to rub Simon the wrong way.

They were sitting in the hayloft of the barn at Simon's place, their legs dangling over the edge, when Simon brought it up again.

"You're really going on another date with that Jackson guy?"

She leaned back, placing her hands behind her as she lifted her face to the sun shining through the large opening. Keeping her eyes shut, she opted to listen to his breathing or the way he was moving before she answered. Just as she expected, the air seemed cooler somehow as soon as he'd brought it up.

"I guess I'm more of the forgiving type, you know? Just because he didn't understand my desire to do interior design doesn't mean he never will." Katrina peeked at him, finding him staring out at the skyline. "Besides, it's just a date. It's not like we're getting married."

"Does *he* know that?" Simon muttered.

She held back a laugh. While his moodiness could be irritating at times, today she was feeling particularly patient. "Didn't Brianne want to set you up on some dates?"

Simon grunted.

"Come on, the girls she knows aren't that bad. You might as well go out with one of them. You never know. What if there's someone out there that has been under your nose this entire time?"

There was no way he didn't pick up on this hint. They'd been spending so much more time together and yet he hadn't even tried to make another move. Katrina was beginning to feel like there was something wrong with her.

"Yeah, I guess you're right."

Her whole body went tight like a stretched-out rubber band, and this time, she looked over to him fully. "Really?"

He didn't meet her gaze at all. His focus remained trained on something outside. Simon used to be so easy to read—mostly because he was always so happy and smiling all the time. As of late, he'd shown a more irritated side of himself about ten percent of the time, and usually when they started talking about Brianne.

Wait a minute. Was Simon grumpy because of their friend? Perhaps it had nothing to do with Katrina dating at all. "Well, then you should come out with us."

Finally, Simon stared at her. "What are you talking about?"

"A bunch of us want to go out as a group this weekend. I'm not sure what we're going to do, but it's probably going to be more fun than sitting around here all day." Katrina studied him, watching for any signs that he might be interested. "I could get Brianne to find someone for you to take." She was reaching again, testing him to see if he was bluffing.

Because while she wasn't completely positive that he might be interested in her—mostly due to her own self-esteem issues—she also wasn't completely sure if it was an issue with Brianne or Jackson.

Or maybe both.

Simon shrugged and turned his focus to the window. "There's a lot of work to do around here. I'm not sure I'd have enough time—"

Katrina bumped against him. "Come on. It will be fun. Lately we haven't been spending a lot of time together—not like we used to." She leaned forward to get a better look at his face. "Is this about Brianne?"

He reacted to that question more than she expected. His body tensed and his brows pulled together. "What are you even talking about?"

"Are you avoiding Brianne? Because it seems like you're a little annoyed with her or something." Then again, he

WHEN YOU'RE FINALLY HOME

might be crushing on her. That would explain why he was avoiding her to a degree.

But Simon had nearly kissed Katrina. Or had he? The memories of that night were getting increasingly cloudy.

Katrina set her focus out the window much like Simon had. "We used to be this trio—spending all our time together, you know?"

"Yeah," he muttered, "but then you moved away. Brianne didn't really spend that much time with me when you weren't here. We only came back together when you got back in town."

She stared at him sharply. "Really?" The strange sense of hope flared back to life in her chest as she studied his features. The muddled feelings she'd been fighting all week were clearing up. Simon could very well have feelings for her, and he was just too scared to do anything about it.

"I don't think you realize that you're the glue that holds our little group together." Simon peeked at her, but only briefly. "Brianne and I don't have a single thing in common. But we both love you."

Her heart stammered.

Love?

Was he confessing his feelings right here, right now?

She blinked a few times, holding her breath for him to say something else that would confirm what he meant by that.

"I mean, how could we not? You guys are like my family and if it wasn't for you, I wouldn't have anyone."

Katrina exhaled slowly through pursed lips. She hadn't realized she'd put her hands in her lap, and she was now clasping them so tightly they were losing all their coloring. They started to tingle, but they weren't the part of her that hurt the most.

Her heart had been squeezed to the point she wasn't sure it was even beating right. Simon had to have feelings for her. All this trying to figure him out was giving her whiplash.

The only issue was that if she was wrong, she'd be humiliated. That, on top of losing her job and being stuck in Rocky Ridge for she didn't know how long, could be the end of her.

"Yeah," she whispered, "I know what you mean. Sometimes I don't feel like I fit in with my family. It's like they were all born to be these great ranchers and cowboys, and I'm just…"

He shifted beside her but didn't say anything. Her chest felt too tight—like she couldn't get enough air.

Katrina sucked in sharply and offered him a wan smile. "I'm just a fish who doesn't belong on land."

"You belong here just as much as anyone else." He placed a hand on her knee and she glanced down. The warmth from his touch was sending shockwaves through her body, telling her that it wasn't just Simon who could be experiencing these feelings. She was very much invested, and if she wasn't willing to admit it to herself, she was going to continue suffering.

WHEN YOU'RE FINALLY HOME

It was too exhausting to have to deal with these sensations for so long.

She'd finally gotten up the courage to just tell him, to ask him what that other night was about, when he spoke first.

"Sure, I'll go out. It's a bonfire? Where's it going to be?"

Her mouth fell open. "Really?"

A spark returned to his eyes—the optimistic guy who could lift her up whenever she found herself too far in the pit of despair. He nodded. "I wouldn't have said so if I wasn't prepared to go. Only, there has to be one condition."

"You name it."

His grin widened. "I'm not coming if we're all going to couple up. I don't want to be set up with anyone. If you can make sure Brianne doesn't turn this into a double date or whatever, then I'll be there."

"Just a bunch of cowboys and cowgirls getting together to throw stuff into a giant fire."

His smile warmed her more than his touch had. Their eyes locked again for a few moments before she blinked and looked away. Now wasn't the time to bring up that kiss. But if he showed any additional signs that he had feelings for her, she wouldn't let him just ignore it.

For now, if he wasn't commenting on it, she wasn't going to push the issue. There had to be a good reason for him to avoid the conversation. And she would let him take the lead.

THE CROWD who showed for the bonfire was bigger than Katrina had expected. There were people she'd never met before. While there were clearly some who were here on a date, Brianne had stuck to her word and told everyone this was just going to be a big party.

Katrina wandered through the groups of people who were chatting as the fire blazed behind her. The heat licked at her, warming her enough that she almost felt overdressed. She'd pulled off her sweatshirt long ago and had tossed it onto a growing pile from others who likely felt the same way.

There was no sign of Simon yet, though he'd promised he'd show up. Brianne was near the snacks and drinks that had been set up on a couple of tables, laughing with someone Katrina recognized as Jackson's friend, making her wonder if Brianne didn't have her own crush developing. That would explain why she was pushing the Duncan cousin so hard. If they both nabbed a guy from the same friend circle, it would make hanging out that much easier.

Katrina grinned as she moved through the growing crowd. One day, they would all be married off and starting their own families. Sometimes that meant friendships got pushed to the back burner, but Katrina knew in her gut she'd never lose what she had with Brianne and Simon.

She slipped between two small groups and collided with someone. Katrina laughed. "I'm so sorry!" Her eyes lifted to find Jackson. "I didn't know you were going to be here this weekend!" She reached forward to give him a hug.

WHEN YOU'RE FINALLY HOME

Jackson lifted her off her feet, his hug nearly crushing her. "When Brianne told me about it, I knew I couldn't miss it." He glanced around, golden flickers from the fire reflecting in his dark eyes. "Wow, you guys really outdid yourselves. I never thought your brother would go for it."

"Who?"

"Bo. I met him at the wedding. He seems really strict." Jackson chuckled. "But then, with a little sister like you... Well, I bet you had a way of getting all your brothers wrapped around your little finger, huh?"

She snickered. "If you believe that, then you don't know my brothers. I think Bo agreed to let this happen because of Gabby, his wife. She can make him say yes to anything. And I think she realized that I needed this."

Jackson cocked his head slightly. "You mean because of the job thing?"

That *job thing* was a big setback. Huge. And still, Jackson didn't seem to fully understand what it had meant to her. Having him downplay something that was a big issue for her right now was more than annoying. Katrina brushed off the annoyance. She was doing her best to show patience and understanding. That was all she could do.

"Yeah. It hit me harder than I thought it would."

"But hasn't it been, like... months?"

She forced a smile. They needed a change of topic. "Tell me how things are going at your family's place. Are you guys still preparing for the rodeo? Or are you going to do something else this summer?"

"Oh yeah. We're going to hit it hard. My little brother is even going to try being a clown."

Katrina couldn't help it, a bout of laughter bubbled up. To hear that a member of the Duncan family was willing to dress in a clown costume to ward off the bulls was hilarious. To see it in person would be priceless.

"You're going to have to tell me when that happens. I wouldn't want to miss it."

Jackson's expression turned slightly more serious and he reached forward to graze his crooked finger along her jawline. "I'd love it if you came with me."

CHAPTER EIGHT

This was it.

Simon knew what he had to do. He had to stop avoiding telling Katrina how he felt. They knew each other better than anyone. It shouldn't be this hard to just admit his feelings to her.

He climbed out of his new beat-up truck and headed straight for the huge fire that burned a few yards away. Somewhere in that group of people, Katrina would be waiting for him. He'd pull her aside and tell her he couldn't get her out of his mind. He couldn't forget about their near-kiss and how he knew he was better than that Jackson Duncan.

He'd tell her that he knew her better than she knew herself and if she gave him a chance, he'd make her the happiest woman alive.

Fueled by this surge of confidence, even though the anxiety brought on by the idea she might brush him off rested just below the surface, he weaved through the crowd.

Then he saw her. Her focus was everywhere all at once. Was she looking for him? He grinned. Now was his moment. All he had to do was go to her and—

A heavy hand landed on his shoulder. "Simon. Katrina said you were going to be here tonight."

Simon dragged his focus to the intruder, finding Daniel smiling at him. He gave a fleeting glance toward Katrina. He needed to make this quick.

"She said you could use some help at the ranch."

He turned to look back at Daniel. "She did?" He'd told Katrina that he would contact Daniel when he was ready. The fact that he hadn't sought him out was because he simply wasn't ready yet.

"Well, she said you would be reaching out when you got to a point you thought I could help." Daniel chuckled. "I thought I'd take the first steps and see what you're interested in."

Simon itched to seek Katrina out but forced himself to continue this conversation. She wouldn't be very pleased with him for brushing off any help her family offered.

"Yeah, um, I wasn't quite ready to give you my questions, but I wanted to get into training. I figured I was pretty good at it with my horses…"

"That's an excellent idea." Daniel folded his arms and moved his feet apart, a clear sign he was in this conversation for the long haul.

Simon couldn't seem to control the way his eyes darted to the side when a familiar figure moved into his peripheral. But she wasn't alone. Simon's whole body went cold. Jackson was talking to her.

Katrina's laugh wasn't hard to pick out from the crowd of people and Simon stiffened further. What was Jackson saying to make her laugh like that?

He turned once again to Daniel. "I guess one of my thoughts was that you'd started your own business. Perhaps you wouldn't mind if I picked your brain one of these days on how you got your clientele."

Daniel shook his head. "You're forgetting that I didn't need clientele. The coffee shop was owned by someone else. I just took it over—sorta the way you took over the dairy farm. But if you want to start offering more services…"

Katrina's laughter once again yanked Simon's attention and he glanced over in time to see Jackson reach out and touch her face.

Fire roared to life in his gut, hotter and more menacing than the one blazing in the darkness before him. He didn't want Jackson touching her. He didn't want them talking to each other. He was going to lose his chance if he didn't just grab the moment.

"I'm sorry, Daniel." He'd probably cut Daniel off, but he hadn't been hearing even half of what he'd been saying. "But Katrina wanted me to find her."

Daniel glanced over to where his sister was and returned his focus to Simon. His eyes narrowed, or at least his expression appeared to be more suspicious than it had before. Then again, Simon's nerves were frayed from the molten feelings that were raging within him and he could be reading into every little nuance of Daniel's expression.

"I'd love to continue this conversation tomorrow morning over coffee if you're available? I heard Megan's stuff is really great."

Daniel gave him a short nod. "I think I can work that into my schedule. Let me give you my number." He held out his hand, and Simon wasted no time in putting his phone there.

He allowed himself one more glance in Katrina's direction, but she'd disappeared. Simon whirled around, his eyes darting back and forth. Where had she gone?

Jackson was missing, too. It wasn't hard to assume that the two of them had slipped off together.

He wasn't proud of where his thoughts were going at this point. If Jackson got up the nerve, he might be the one to steal that coveted kiss. Simon's stomach swirled. He had to find her.

The second Daniel returned the phone to his hand, Simon darted away. He wasn't proud of how he pushed through groups of people. Several called out to him to be careful, and he tossed a few apologies over his shoulder.

Still no sign of Katrina.

Dang it! He'd had all week to talk to her about how he felt and he'd blown it sky high.

"Hey, where's the fire?" Brianne sidled up beside him and nudged him with her elbow, laughing.

If he was in a better mood, he might have played along with her ridiculous statement. "Have you seen Katrina? She wanted me to meet her here."

"I'm sure she's around here somewhere." Brianne's eyes danced through the crowd, with practically no direction. "Have you tried calling her yet?"

"I doubt she'd be able to hear her phone with all the noise going on."

"Yeah, you're probably right. Well, she'll turn up. She probably just got caught up with someone else."

"That's what I'm afraid of," he muttered.

"What?" Brianne called back.

"I need to find her before I leave."

"You're leaving already?" Her wide eyes landed on him with accusation. "You're the reason she made me promise not to make this a couples thing. You can't just leave."

"Sure I can. I don't like these sorts of things."

Brianne lifted a brow and folded her arms. "Liar. I know for a fact you're one of the more social people around here. You might not date much, but you would have never been hired as a waiter at that restaurant if you weren't good with people."

He sighed. She was right, of course. But he couldn't handle being here with Katrina if she was going to slip out into the night with someone else.

"You okay? You look… sorta sick."

"Why do you think I want to leave?"

"Well, you could have just said so." Still, Brianne seemed to be studying him more than she usually did. Her eyes were narrowed and she moved a little closer. "Can I ask you something? Why *don't* you date?"

He gawked at her. What kind of question was that?

"You don't have to answer, but you're clearly a catch. You're sweet and you work hard. But you're only ever hanging out with me and Katrina." Her eyes grew wide. "Unless you already have your eye on someone and you don't want us to know. Is she long distance? Have you been dating someone, and you haven't told us about her?" She whacked him playfully. "How could you not tell us!"

"Brianne, no. I'm not involved with anyone, local or otherwise." He turned his search outward again as he continued speaking. "I'm too busy for that sort of thing. I'd rather spend my free time with the people I know and care about rather than try to play the dating game with someone new. I don't have the patience for that."

She snorted. "Yeah, that doesn't sound right. You're social. You don't have to play the *game*. It's something else and I know it. You don't have to tell me, but I'll figure it out anyway." Brianne turned away from him. "It's sweet, you know. The way you're helping Katrina out so much. I think she's doing a lot better, don't you?"

"Yeah, maybe," he mumbled.

"I bet it has a lot to do with you keeping her busy at your farm." She said this quieter, but he heard every word.

"And I bet it hasn't hurt to get her out and dating." This time, Brianne glanced at him. "You know I'm right even if you don't like it."

"I never said I didn't like it. I'm just swamped. I don't need to hear about her dating escapades." And he didn't need to witness them, either. Simon heaved a sigh. "If you see her, tell her that I stopped by but couldn't find her."

"Find who?"

Both Simon and Brianne spun around, but Brianne acted quicker. She threw her arms around Katrina. "There you are!" When she pulled back, she gave her an annoying grin and wagged her brows. "I saw you with Jackson. Did you two... have a nice chat?"

Katrina glanced at Simon, but he looked away. "We were just chatting about the rodeo. Did you know his younger brother wants to be one of those clowns that distracts the bull?"

Brianne laughed. "That's awesome. Dangerous, though. Is he going to be fast enough?"

"I hope so." Katrina nudged Simon, drawing his attention. "When did you get here? I was looking for you."

All his drive and determination to tell her exactly how he felt had disappeared. She hadn't been looking for him. She'd been happily engaged in her conversation with Jackson. Heck, Brianne had said herself that Jackson lived close enough to the city that she could still work there while being married to a cowboy. Simon couldn't let himself forget that little nugget of information.

Katrina wanted nothing to do with Rocky Ridge, and that was where Simon would be spending the rest of his life.

He flashed her a smile, doing his best to make her believe he wasn't upset in the slightest. "Just got here."

"Yeah, and he said he was just leaving," Brianne teased.

Katrina's eyes shot to meet his, accusation emanating from them. "What?"

He shrugged. "It's not what I thought it would be. Don't you think it's a little too... *country*?" Even to him, the tone of his voice seemed to take a dig at the folks who preferred living here. "But you understand about that. You don't like being here either."

Her mouth fell open and she let out a surprised laugh. "Simon!"

"It's true though, right? You want your career. You're still putting in applications. What does Jackson think about that?"

She snickered, clearly in a better mood than he was. He needed to step up his game if he didn't want to get pulled aside and given a lecture.

"Actually, yeah. He said he thinks I should do what makes me happy." She glanced toward Brianne and back to Simon. "And I've been thinking a lot about it lately."

Brianne made a whooping sound. "Are you saying what I think you're saying? You might actually settle down with a cowboy? Are you guys dating?"

Simon couldn't move. This was it. He'd waited too long. He'd been a coward, and he only had himself to blame.

WHEN YOU'RE FINALLY HOME

Katrina gave Brianne a pointed look. "No, I'm not dating Jackson. Though, I have to admit that while I never really saw myself with a cowboy before..." Her eyes flitted up to meet Simon's briefly. "I might actually be warming up to it."

She didn't just say that.

Did she?

Katrina was warming up to the idea of being with a cowboy.

Simon was a cowboy.

Well, he was one now. And Katrina wasn't dating Jackson. Simon still had a shot with her. If he could get her alone sometime tonight, he might have a second chance.

Katrina reached up and stole the hat from his head, placing it on her own. "What do you think, guys? Would I make a good farmer's wife?" She winked at Brianne, who let out another whoop.

"You know it!"

They both laughed and Katrina pulled his hat off to hand it to him. He shook his head. "It suits you better than it suits me."

It almost looked like she was trying to hide her smile. Her eyes bounced up to meet his briefly as she returned the hat to her head. "Thanks."

CHAPTER NINE

When most of the guests had taken off and it was only Simon, Brianne, Katrina, and her brothers remaining, they started to clean up. There wasn't much in the way of trash, thankfully, as the folks around here did a good job at aiming for the garbage cans.

Brianne was the first to head out after most of the area was picked up. Then Wade and Bo took the garbage bins back to the house. Finally, the only ones left were Simon and Katrina.

They wandered toward the house, their steps slow and measured. Simon was unusually quiet, but she wasn't going to put up with that. Katrina glanced toward him, taking the hat from her head and offering it to him again.

"It was fun to wear for the night, but I'm guessing you're going to need it back."

Simon shook his head. "I don't need it. I've got a couple more." He took the hat from her hands and placed it on her head again. "Besides, I wasn't lying when I said that you look better in it than I do."

She smiled, striking a pose. "Like this?"

He chuckled, and she could see that happy guy she knew beneath it all.

"I'm really glad you came tonight. I didn't realize how busy it was going to be. I can't believe Brianne knows so many people."

"Parties like this one might start off with everyone being invited by someone you know, but then it grows. I would wager that several people here tonight invited their friends. You're just lucky the folks you started with were respectable people and this one didn't get out of hand."

"You're probably right." She made a face. "Can you imagine how Bo would have reacted if this party had gone off the rails? I still can't believe he was on board with this. Though it does make sense he'd stick around 'til the end."

The conversation was so awkward. She wanted to discuss so much more than the party. At this point, she would have loved it if he confessed that he wanted to take her out. After spending more time with Jackson, she'd realized that he simply wasn't boyfriend material. He was fun to hang out with, but he wasn't Simon.

Her heart hammered as she glanced up at her best friend. Something that should have been so easy to talk about was probably the hardest thing she would ever have to bring up. She took a deep breath and steeled herself to do just that when he cut her off.

"I saw you talking to Jackson."

Katrina's breath caught in her throat and she started coughing. It took her a moment to settle before she could finally find her voice and even then, it was more of a wheeze. "You did?"

"Yeah. Seems he's getting on your good side, huh? I'd bet Brianne is excited about that."

"Why would she be?" Her thoughts immediately went to the cowboy she'd been chatting up earlier in the evening. Had Simon seen that, too? Was he under the assumption that his two friends were conspiring to find men they could date together?

A chill ran down her spine. If he thought she wasn't interested, that would explain why he wasn't speaking up.

"Because she wants to be the one to help you find the guy you're meant to marry." He said it simply enough, but there was a weight to his voice that threw her off. It almost sounded like he wanted to be the one to help her through what she'd been dealing with.

Katrina stopped and placed a hand on his forearm. "I want you to know that whatever happens, I'm indebted to you."

His expression didn't change. He studied her with the kind of gaze that could drill deep into her soul and read her thoughts, making it hard for her to maintain eye contact.

"When I came back here, I was devastated. I had worked my whole life for something I'd wanted more than anything in the world. I couldn't see past that pain even if my family's lives depended on it." She swallowed hard. This wasn't the way she'd wanted this conversation to go.

Not by a long shot. "But you and Brianne helped me get through it. You guys did it in different ways, but I wouldn't be where I am without either of you."

He worked his jaw. Even in the moonlight, she could see every angle of his face. Had he been wearing his hat, it might have been harder for her to read him. Heck, it was hard enough as it was, but at least now she could see his features soften slightly.

"Brianne just has a different way of doing things. And I'm not ready to get into anything serious, anyway. She keeps pushing me to Jackson like she expects me to declare my love for him and get engaged tomorrow." Katrina let out a nervous laugh. "But that's not going to happen."

"You don't know that," he murmured. One side of his mouth quirked upward and he glanced away, his brows pulling together. "So, you don't think you're ready for a relationship…"

That wasn't exactly what she'd meant. She didn't think she was ready to get engaged any time soon, but she wouldn't say no if Simon would just ask her out. Would they get married tomorrow? No, of course not. But at least she'd be able to see if all these strange feelings were real or if they were just wishful thinking.

She looked down to where she was still touching his arm and pulled back. "I'm not interested in a serious relationship with Jackson, that's for sure. He's trying. I can tell he's making an effort…" A small smile touched her lips as she considered the conversation she'd had with him. "But he's still a little clueless. I think it's because he grew up in the country his whole life."

Simon shifted and she looked up to find him watching her. "We've all grown up in the country. You have, too." His tone held a bit of a bite.

"That's not what I mean." Great, now she was flustered. "What I mean is that he doesn't see the value of being anywhere else. He hasn't gone anywhere or done anything outside of the small town where he grew up."

Simon's expression hardened further. "I haven't either."

The heat in her face intensified. "Yeah, but you're different."

"How am I different?" he demanded. "Because based on what you just said about Jackson, none of the guys in this area are going to be good enough. If you're only interested in the guys back where you were working, then maybe you need to stop spending time around the bonfire and start hunting harder for that job you want so much."

She gaped at him, her eyes wide. Somewhere along the line, she'd struck a chord with what she'd said. And now she couldn't think of anything to combat what he'd told her.

Katrina threw up her hands and marched past him. "I can't do this tonight, Simon."

She'd only made it five steps before she heard his boots hitting the ground, following her.

Simon's hand wrapped around her forearm and he pulled her to a stop.

She blinked several times with surprise, her eyes darting to meet his, then looking away, then back. "What do you want from me, Simon? Whatever it is that's bothering you has to stop because I'm having a hard enough time as it is. Some days, you're cold and irritable. Others, you're the same old happy Simon. And then there are the days when I swear…"

She looked away again, not sure if she could voice the feelings she'd been experiencing in her gut.

"If there's something I did to offend you, just tell me."

"You haven't offended me," he bit out. "But I can't bear to watch you in limbo anymore. You're right. I was there when you lost your job and came home. I was there when you didn't want to leave your room and all you wanted to do was apply for job after job. I was there when you needed to get out of the house and made sure you did. I'm always there for you."

She waited, expecting him to continue, to get to the point so they could hash everything out. But apparently, that was where he wanted to end his statement. Katrina huffed, yanking her arm out of his grasp, but she didn't storm away like she might have done years ago. Instead, she marched right up to him, her face inches from his.

"I might be in limbo, but you're bouncing around so much you're giving me whiplash. I don't understand what's wrong. Tell me so we can just be friends again."

As much as she wanted to test the waters and see where these feelings might lead, it had been emotionally draining, not knowing where she stood. Waiting for him to make that first move.

Even now, he was hesitating, holding back. She could sense it. More than sense it, she could see it in the way his eyes flickered with varying degrees of emotion.

Well, if he wasn't going to do anything about it, she would.

Her focus shifted to his mouth, and the way it was pressed into a firm, thin line. Here was her shot. There would be no interruptions. She could just take his face between her hands and kiss him, right here, right now. Then he wouldn't be able to run away from it.

"Simon," she whispered, "just tell me what you're thinking."

One of his eyes twitched and he exhaled. "I want you to be happy, Katrina. That's all this has ever been about."

Her stomach flipped. *Then help me make that happen*.

The words had formed in her head; they were practically on her lips. She closed her eyes and leaned closer to him. Then it was like time had sped up. Something strange happened where one moment Simon was in front of her about to be kissed, and the next he was a few feet away.

"It's getting late, and your brothers are bound to come looking for you if you don't head inside." He nodded toward the house behind her. She hadn't even realized they were this close.

Everything up until this point seemed to have been shrouded by a cloud, muddled by the fog. Katrina didn't even have a chance to make sense of what had happened before Simon waved and headed toward his truck.

"I'll see you Monday," he called over his shoulder.

Fury boiled within her. This was the second time she'd been left hanging. All of the anticipation from that last near-kiss had culminated into a massive ball of pain and anger. Was her judgment so bad she'd been reading into everything when it came to Simon? Had she seen signs that were simply not there?

The least he could have done was physically stop her from nearly kissing him rather than walking away. What kind of guy did that?

"I want you to be happy," she mimicked with sarcasm. "Limbo!" She threw her hands into the air again. "What does that even mean?" She called the words out to everyone and no one. She shouted them at the sky and her frustration continued to grow. "I'm not in limbo. I still plan to get back on my feet. I'm just taking the scenic route."

She was well aware that she sounded like a crazy person, outside in the dark talking to herself, but she had no one else. Brianne wouldn't believe her if she said that Simon had been sending her mixed signals. And even if she did, she would probably not approve in the slightest.

Katrina growled and stomped her way into the house. Well, if Simon was going to keep messing with her this way, then he clearly wasn't interested. She had her answer. She might as well let Brianne find her someone else to go on a date with. Jackson wasn't a good option, though he could be sweet when he really wanted to be.

What Katrina needed was someone who knew what they wanted and wasn't afraid to actually do something about it. She had no idea what Simon wanted. And she was done playing games.

She hurried to her room, avoiding any interaction with her family. Pulling out her phone, she dialed her friend.

Brianne answered on the first ring.

"Find someone else for me to go on a date with."

"What about Jackson?"

"He's nice and all, but we're just not clicking. There's no…" She thought about Simon and the way he could make her feel just by looking at her. She wanted that, but with someone who would help it grow. "Spark. I want a spark."

There was a pause on the other end of the line. "I know what you mean. Let me see what I can come up with, okay? I'll get back to you."

"Great." Katrina hung up the phone and tossed it onto her bed. After tonight, Simon had better be nicer to her. She was finally going after something that would make her happy.

Hopefully.

CHAPTER TEN

SIMON SLAMMED HIS TRUCK DOOR A LITTLE TOO HARD, grimacing when the vehicle shook. He paced outside of his house, not ready to feel confined. He was an idiot. That much was clear.

And a coward.

And a bad friend.

And every rotten name in the book.

Katrina deserved so much better. What was holding him back? He'd been so ready to just lay everything out on the table and tell her they should take a chance on being together, no matter the consequences.

But seeing how happy she'd been with Jackson had made him realize she needed someone who could do that for her while still having a friend like him around to reel her in.

He raked his hands through his hair and let out a groan. Something told him that he couldn't be both. If he crossed the line from friendship to boyfriend, he wouldn't be able to cross back. So when she clearly wanted him to kiss her, he'd choked.

She didn't know what she wanted. She'd probably just been caught up in the moment she'd had with Jackson, and it was bleeding into the conversation they were having.

That made a lot more sense than her trying to make something happen between the two of them.

Simon slowed his pacing, allowing his thoughts to mull over the evening and what exactly he was feeling. There was no doubt that he had feelings for her. If Jackson wasn't an issue, if her dream career wasn't in jeopardy, then he would have told her about his feelings.

At least, he liked to think he would have.

There was no telling at this point. Looking at his history, he clearly couldn't handle telling her anything like that. The closest he'd gotten was telling her she deserved better and that he wanted her to be happy.

Worn out from the adrenaline that had brought him here, he settled down on the bottom step. He sat there for a few minutes until a pair of headlights flashed onto his property. There was zero chance this was a good thing. If it was someone he knew, they would have called.

Unless they wanted to catch him off guard so he couldn't take off and leave the conversation they were forcing on him.

He got to his feet, alarm bells ringing in his head. This was definitely not a good thing. In the dark, he couldn't even tell who the car belonged to. All he knew was that it wasn't a truck. That meant the person approaching was probably from town rather than the surrounding ranches. Simon leaned against the railing at his back and steeled himself for whatever was about to happen.

The car came to a stop and the driver didn't even bother shutting off the engine before shoving the door open and marching toward him.

His shoulders relaxed but only somewhat. Brianne didn't have any reason to stop by unannounced. While they were close enough, they simply didn't have the friendship that he had with Katrina.

That thought alone pushed him back into fight-or-flight mode. He pulled away from the porch and met Brianne in front of her car's headlights.

"What's the matter? Is it Katrina?"

Without preamble, she lifted both hands and pushed him. He stumbled back a step.

"What was that for?" he demanded.

"You're an idiot."

He had done everything he could to prevent himself from showing his cards. If Katrina had spoken to Brianne, then this was worse than he'd thought. What could she have said that would get Brianne this upset? He could only imagine the conversation they might have had just before Brianne drove over here.

Still, he refused to say a single word until he knew what he was dealing with.

She shook her head and paced in front of her car. "I can't believe I didn't see it sooner."

His eyes watched her. Back and forth. Back and forth.

"Here I was trying to find out why Katrina wasn't going for Jackson even though they're *perfect* for each other and I come to find out it's because of *you!*" She pulled herself up short and pointed a finger at him. Her eyes flashed with fury. "What do you have to say for yourself?"

"I'm sorry?"

"That doesn't sound like an apology."

"That's because it isn't," he muttered gruffly. "I get that we're friends and all, but you can't stand there accusing me of something when I have no idea what you're talking about."

"Katrina and Jackson. She's not interested in him."

"That's because he's terrible for her."

Brianne groaned. "No, he's not. He's perfect. He's got the ranching know-how like her brothers, and he lives close enough to the city—"

"Proximity doesn't make him perfect for her," Simon interjected. "Haven't you been paying attention? Katrina wants someone who's interested in helping her achieve her dreams. She wants someone who will listen to her and tell her that she can still do what she wants to with her life. Jackson is an idiot. He might be good-looking, and he might know his way around a tractor, but he's not interested in her the way she needs him to be."

"And who is? You?"

The accusation in her voice cut through him like a knife.

"I never said—"

"You didn't have to." She placed her hands on her hips as she glowered at him. "You're supposed to be her *friend*, Simon. That means you can't fall in love with her."

He froze. In the dark, with the lights at her back, he was sure she could see his expression and just how shocked he was that she'd figured out his secret. Unfortunately, he had no way of seeing her face clearly enough to know if she was bluffing.

It didn't matter anyway, because she'd caught him. He didn't know how, but she'd figured everything out. The only question was if Katrina knew. Heart pumping faster than it had in his entire life, Simon wished he could read Brianne's mind—to know what exactly had been shared between the woman he loved and her best friend.

"I *knew* it! Geez, Simon. How could you?"

"How could I what? I haven't done anything!"

"You fell in love with your best friend." She dragged a hand down her face. "Do you know how stupid that was? If you guys don't work out, what then? Do you think life will ever feel normal again? There's an unspoken rule that you can't date your best friend."

"I didn't do anything!" he snapped again. "I didn't tell her I liked her. I didn't kiss her. I didn't—"

"You might as well have!" She marched closer. "Whether you like it or not, you did something, and now she can't get you out of her mind."

"Is that what she told you?" His voice was quieter, and he could hear the hopefulness shining through. As much as he hated that he was confessing everything to Brianne, he couldn't deny how this information pleased him.

"Of course not!"

That caught him off guard and he stiffened. "What?"

"She didn't have to," Brianne continued. "She called me after I left and told me to set her up with someone else."

Disappointment washed over him like a tidal wave, taking with it his stomach and lungs. He was being swept up in a storm and he was drowning. "She did?"

"I can only assume you did something after I left. At first, I thought that you'd kissed her… or that she kissed you and you turned her down. But then I realized that she would have told me if that had happened. But I knew something weird was going on between you. I just had to see the look on your face to confirm it."

"Well, you can rest assured that nothing will happen between us." Saying the words out loud made him feel sick to his stomach. "Is that what you came here to do? To make demands and ensure that Katrina and I will never become a thing?"

Still, her hands were on her hips. Her hard stare remained fixed on him, pinning him in place. Then, slowly, she shook her head and her hands dropped to her sides. "No."

WHEN YOU'RE FINALLY HOME

"Then what do you want from me? I didn't do anything wrong. I've been fighting these feelings for the last several weeks. You should be thanking me for staying out of it."

She huffed.

"What do you want?" he demanded again.

"I don't know. But she's upset and you made me a promise when she got back that we would get her back on track. What happened to that plan? Huh? She was doing so great…" Her eyes shifted to the side, staring at nothing. "She… really was," Brianne murmured quietly. Then her gaze flitted back to meet his. "She was doing better because of you."

"I wasn't doing anything. I just let her help out with my farm."

Brianne moved closer still. "No, she was spending time with you. I was telling the truth when I said she couldn't stop thinking about you. It's all coming together. Katrina likes you, too."

"It doesn't matter," he hedged. "Like you said, it's against the friend code. We can't—"

She sliced her hand through the air, waving him off. "That was when we were in high school. Who cares what happens now? For the last several years, she wasn't even living in Montana. What if all she needs is somewhere to feel like home again?" Brianne was rambling more to herself than to him and he knew it. She wanted Katrina to stay just as much as he did.

Her eyes shot to meet his and she smiled widely.

Simon shook his head. "I know that look. You're planning something."

"And you're going to be on board the second you hear what I have to say."

He held up both hands and let out a worried chuckle. "I don't want to play any games."

"It's not a game, Simon." She rubbed her hands together. "She wants to date someone who gives her that spark. And that's you."

"You don't know that," he argued. "She hasn't said a single thing to make me believe she's interested."

"So? Maybe she's waiting for you to do that." She hopped up on the balls of her feet. "You're going on a date with her!"

"What? No, I'm not."

"Yes, you are. You're going to tell her you have feelings for her and you're going to see if she feels the same way."

He gaped at her. This plan was a very bad idea. Brianne could be wrong. Then he'd be putting his heart out there and Katrina could turn him down, leaving him broken and alone.

"That's a bad idea."

She gave his shoulder a little shove. "Of course it is. But you started it. And if you don't tell her, I will."

If his eyes weren't already bugging out of his head, they were now. "You wouldn't."

"Oh yes, I would. She hasn't found a new job yet, and she's actually asking for my help to go out with someone else. You're helping me with this one or I'm telling."

"Now you just sound like you want to punish me."

She shrugged and her smile widened. "Maybe you deserve it."

Simon crossed his arms and took a step back. For the first time since Katrina had come back to town, he was putting his foot down. Brianne couldn't boss him around and he wasn't going to be the one to actually ruin his friendship with the one girl he'd always cared for. "Do what you're going to do. I'm not going to be your puppet."

This time, her mouth fell open. "Seriously?" She threw back her head and groaned again. "What is wrong with you?" When her angry eyes found his, they were narrowed into slits. "Do you love her?"

"Of course I do."

"No, I mean do you *really* love her? Like, when you look into a crystal ball and visualize your future, is Katrina the woman you see yourself with?"

The answer was on his lips before he had a chance to rein it in. "Yes."

"Then stop dragging your feet and *do* something about it. You've never been one to shy away from anything. You jumped in on this ranch thing, didn't you? I bet you didn't even think twice about it when you got the call."

"So?"

"So," she drawled, "if you knew for certain that Katrina feels the same way about you that you feel about her, would you ask her out?"

"Yes," he muttered, hating the way Brianne was starting to make a great deal of sense.

"Then be at The Steer House tomorrow night at five sharp. Tell Katrina how you feel and don't leave until you get your answers." She spun on her heels and headed back for her car. She stopped before ducking inside. "It's funny, you know?"

"What?"

"I've seen you go on dates with girls. In high school, you never had any issues asking them out. You had all the confidence in the world. Now that I know you like her, everything makes more sense."

Simon sighed. "I have no idea what you're talking about."

"People hesitate more when they're scared of losing something. I don't think I've ever seen *you* scared of losing anything."

"I feel like you're trying to make a point here."

She shrugged. "I guess what I'm trying to say is that Katrina is the one thing you care about most." Brianne waited for a moment as if expecting him to respond. He didn't have anything he could say to that statement—mostly because he'd never considered it before.

Finally, she climbed in her car, shut the door, and drove away.

She was absolutely right.

If there was one thing in his life he would be devastated to lose, it wouldn't be his farm, it wouldn't be his home, it wouldn't even be his own life.

It was Katrina.

And that was why he couldn't wait until tomorrow night to see her.

CHAPTER ELEVEN

This was the right thing to do.

That was what Katrina kept telling herself as she sat on the edge of her bed, lacking the energy to get ready for bed. She stared off at the corner of her room, feeling sorry for herself and hating that she'd come to this point of her life again.

Why couldn't she be like Simon? He had a natural way of being able to find joy in the simplest of things. Well, that wasn't entirely true. Lately, he wasn't as happy as he used to be. That could be due to the stress of his new career path, or it could be the issues he might have been having with Brianne.

As if just the thought of her friend was enough to summon her, she got a call. Katrina stared at the screen as her friend's name scrolled across the top. She didn't want to hear that Brianne had already found someone for her to go out with. Did she have someone in her back pocket waiting for this exact situation or something?

She heaved a sigh, trying to push the frustration aside. Of course she'd found someone. She was the queen of matchmaking.

Katrina pushed the phone aside. Brianne would just assume that she was in the shower or that she was getting ready for bed. They could talk in the morning. She fell back on her bed and stared at the ceiling, contemplating what would have happened if she'd just gone after Simon and told him to kiss her like she'd wanted him to.

A smile tugged at her lips. She would have loved to see the surprised look on his face. If it worked out like it did in the movies, then he would have kissed her back and they would have laughed over how it had taken them this long to finally figure out that they had feelings for each other.

Her smile faded as she reached for a pillow and hugged it to her chest. It could have gone the other way, too. He might have had to physically push her away and remind her where they stood—as *friends*.

That was practically what he'd done tonight, wasn't it? He'd basically run away from her. And that was the reason she knew she was making the right choice. This was what she had to do to stay sane.

A tap on her window drew her attention and she glanced over at the glass. It was dark outside and her light was on; maybe a moth had rammed into the window. Katrina turned her attention back to the ceiling. As long as Simon remained her friend, she'd be happy. He was her rock.

Another tap on her window, this time louder, caused her to jump, and she rolled onto her side before sliding off the bed and approaching it with curiosity. Another tap. She paused, startled. Then she hurried forward and pulled open the blinds. It was too dark to see anything through the pane.

With a grunt, she pushed the window open and leaned out.

Immediately, she saw the shadowy figure down below. Simon's face peered up at her from the darkness. She squinted and let out a strangled laugh.

"Simon? What are you doing here?"

He shrugged.

She laughed again. "You came all the way back... did you forget something?"

Simon looked away then brought his eyes back to her before running a hand through his hair. "I wanted to talk to you about something."

Her heart stumbled. This could be about anything. While he didn't sound mad, she refused to get her hopes up that he was here for what she wanted. She swallowed hard, a smile spreading across her face though it felt like the most unnatural thing at this moment.

She crossed her arms and leaned on the ledge of the window. "What did you want to talk about?"

He shifted and looked away again. With each passing second, it was getting harder and harder for her to believe this wasn't exactly what she wanted it to be. She could feel her heart thrum in her chest at a frequency that was definitely not natural.

"Will you come down? I would really like to speak to you face to face."

Katrina brought up her finger to her chin and tapped it a little. "You know, I've just gotten ready for bed. I really don't want to have to come down there in the cold. Whatever it is, I'm sure you could just—"

"For Pete's sake, Katrina! Will you get down here so we can have this discussion like adults?"

Her eyes widened, his sharp tone unexpected. There was a good chance she was wrong and all this teasing would only humiliate her further. "Is everything okay?" she asked, realizing all at once that if this wasn't a big deal, he could have called her or texted her.

Simon stared at her hard, expectant. He'd made his request and if she was any kind of friend, she'd have been down there five minutes ago. Then his features softened. His eyes delved into hers in such a way that she nearly melted right then and there.

"I just… need to talk."

She nodded. "I'll be right down."

With each step she took, her legs shook. By the time she made it outside, her hands were trembling, too. Katrina hurried down the steps and toward the side of the building. Darting around the corner, she nearly collided with Simon.

His hands shot out, grasping her upper arms to keep her at arm's length. The porch light was too far away to do much good, so all she had was the glow from the moon overhead to study his features.

Simon's jaw was tight, and his eyes were serious. Whatever his reason for being here now, it was important.

"Are you okay?" she finally found her voice enough to whisper.

His gaze searched hers as he worked his jaw back and forth. "I need you to know something."

Her pulse quickened, ripping her through loops and over hills into the depths of the lowest valleys like she were on a death-defying roller coaster. But lately, that was how Simon affected her. He had a way of making her question everything she wanted in life and at the same time helped her know exactly what she wanted.

And she wanted him.

Her whole body flushed then went cold, causing a stampede of shivers to tear down her spine. "Okay," she mumbled.

"When I think about the person who makes me the most happy, it's you."

She gave him a shy smile. "You make me feel happy, too."

His hands tightened on her, and he shook his head. "No, this is more than that. I…" He took a deep breath and released it with force. Simon shut his eyes and muttered a curse. When he opened his eyes, they were blazing with what could only be described as desire.

Her heart leaped into her throat. Before she had a chance to react, he released her only to grasp her chin and pull her toward him.

Simon's kiss was soft and sweet at first. It was almost timid. But that didn't last long. The second she reacted under his touch, his hold on her grew more urgent. His kiss became frantic and passionate.

It was as if his heart were speaking to her, demanding that she give herself and everything she knew to him. They were two halves of a whole that had been split when the earth began and now, they'd finally found each other.

She pushed her hands into his hair, clinging to him, kissing him with every ounce of her being. This was a man who had always been there for her. He'd been the one to push her toward her dreams no matter how hard it was. He'd lifted her when she couldn't stand on her own and he'd forced her to be the best version of herself.

Simon was the reason she'd left for college out of state, and he'd been here to pick up the pieces when she'd come back home.

He was the source of her strength, and it wasn't until this moment she fully appreciated all of that. And when he held her like she was the exact same thing for him, she knew she'd found the spark she'd been looking for.

It had been right under her nose.

Simon was the first to pull back, causing her to nearly fall into him without the support he offered. Her lashes fluttered and she exhaled, despite feeling like there wasn't any oxygen left in her lungs.

He pressed his forehead against hers. Their breaths mingled in the air between them, that being the only sound besides the usual indication that they were surrounded by nature.

Crickets continued chirping. The breeze rustled the leaves of the nearby trees. Grass reeds swayed along with everything else as if the world hadn't completely turned upside down on its axis.

When he didn't speak after a while, she knew she had to say something.

"Are you okay?" she whispered. He had to be reeling, too. What were they supposed to do now? Pandora's box had officially been opened and now she wasn't sure if they'd be able to put everything back.

He nodded, then let out another heavy breath. "Being with you this way is completely terrifying."

She forced a laugh—what else could she do? "Those words don't instill a great deal of confidence after being kissed by your best friend."

Simon hooked his finger beneath her chin again and grazed her lips with his before setting a firm gaze on her. "Out of everyone in my life, I would never want to lose you. That kind of regret would tear me up from the inside out."

She understood. She felt the same way. All it would take is for them to have a bad breakup for there to be undeniable regret. Their friendship was the one thing she still loved about coming home. And now it was in jeopardy.

She refused to think that way. There was no sense in borrowing trouble. "I would prefer to call it exhilarating."

Finally, he smiled. "That too." His hand slipped behind her neck and he pulled her close, letting her rest her cheek on his chest. "I fought this so hard. Every single day has been utter torture."

She smiled, pulling her lower lip between her teeth. "You really have a way with words."

He chuckled, the vibrations reverberating through his chest and making her laugh. Simon wrapped his arms around her, preventing her from being able to get very far. "I'm a little out of practice."

"How about you just say that you've wanted to kiss me like that since the day I came back?"

"I've wanted to kiss you since the day we met," he murmured.

He was telling the truth. How had she not noticed? How had she been so blind as to not see that his feelings for her had been there this entire time?

"Don't look at me like that."

"But—"

He shook his head, grazing her cheek with his knuckles. "It was never right for you."

"You can't say that."

"Sure, I can. How many times did you tell me that you wanted to move to New York when we were kids?"

She snapped her mouth shut.

"How many times did you tell me you hated living in a town where everyone knew you?"

This time, she bit down on her lips, thinning them. He was right—again.

"I wasn't going to stand in your way. It's like I said. I just want you to be happy."

CHAPTER TWELVE

It couldn't be this easy.

All this time, Simon had fretted over destroying something, over losing something. In the grand scheme of things, he'd had nothing to worry about. He'd overthought until he'd made himself sick.

That was the old Simon. And the old Simon would have looked at all that time as time he'd wasted when he could have just stepped up and gotten everything he wanted.

Better late than never.

As he held Katrina, right here, right now, he vowed he wouldn't be the one to stand in his own way. She was too important to him and none of this would have happened if Brianne hadn't told him to go out with her tomorrow.

Simon groaned, startling Katrina enough that she pulled away from him. She stared up at him with concern, wrinkles marring her forehead. "What's the matter?"

He shook his head. The last thing she needed was to hear that he hadn't been brave enough to come here without Brianne's help. Already he could imagine what she would say or what she might do. It wasn't so far-fetched to think that Katrina might also have doubts about them.

Heck, she might even wonder if he and Brianne had planned this whole thing from the beginning.

Shoot! He should probably tell Brianne to play it cool. Better yet, he might want to tell her to pretend to be surprised. It would hurt for her to throw the same kind of fit in front of Katrina when they inevitably talked.

Katrina peered up at him, forcing him to come back to the present. He cupped her face with his palm and brushed his thumb across her cheekbone. "It's nothing. I just realized I have to call Brianne about something."

Her eyes rounded larger than he thought possible. A gasp tore from her throat and she darted backward, but he caught her hand in time to stop her. "Now it's your turn. What's going on?"

She blushed. Even without the sun shining, he could see the deep color spreading from ear to ear. "I don't think you're going to like it."

"That definitely doesn't sound good."

Katrina returned to his side. She gnawed on her lower lip as she grabbed his hand and fidgeted with his fingers. "I don't want you to get upset, but I told her to set me up with someone new."

He lifted his brows, but it was only for show.

"I know." She grimaced. "What do you think she's going to say when I tell her that whoever she found is going to have to cancel?"

"Are you sure she found someone? It hasn't been very long."

Her eyes drifted toward the house and she nodded. "I'm sure. She wouldn't have called me so late if she hadn't found someone to take me out. I didn't answer her call, but I'm positive that she did."

"How?"

Katrina swung her attention back to him. "She never leaves voice messages. And one popped up right before you got here."

Wow. He had to hand it to her; Brianne was good at what she did. If anyone could have found a replacement love interest, it would be her. He itched to just tell her, to let her know that Brianne had been one step ahead of both of them, and he was the one Brianne would push in Katrina's direction.

Holding his tongue on this little tidbit was proving to be harder than hiding his feelings for Katrina in the first place. "You should probably call her back."

She shot him a sharp look. "I can't do that."

"Why not?"

Her flat look was almost comedic. If he wasn't absolutely certain he was the prospective boyfriend, he might have worn a similar expression.

Now that he knew he had everything he could ever want, his positive outlook had returned in full force. Rather than ask Brianne to keep their little meeting a secret, she could continue pushing Katrina to go on that date tomorrow and they would both surprise her.

Katrina continued worrying her lower lip. She shifted her weight from one foot to the other and let out a heavy breath. "I think she's gonna be mad."

"Why?"

"Will you stop asking me that? This is Brianne. She isn't going to be thrilled that we're…"

"That we're what?" He bit back a smile when she glared at him.

"I don't know what we're doing."

"You don't?"

Katrina groaned. "Seriously, stop asking questions. She's gonna feel like the third wheel if we start seeing each other. On top of that, whoever she just found for me is going to expect to go on a date and Brianne will be furious if I make her look bad and cancel." She lifted her gaze to his. "What do we do?"

Simon took both of her hands in his and offered her the most reassuring smile he could muster. "I think you see what's in your voicemail. Then I think you go on that date—"

"Absolutely not!"

"Hear me out." He caressed her face once more, absolutely loving how nice it was to not need an excuse to do just that. "If you go out with the guy, then you can say you're not interested without being rude. Brianne won't feel like you disregarded the hard work she put into finding him. And you can figure out if this is what you really want."

There was a fleeting moment when he could have sworn he saw some pain in her expression. But just as quickly as it had appeared, it was gone.

"You want me to go on a date with another guy... someone who isn't you?" The disbelief in her voice was only outshined by the ache just beneath the surface.

He cringed at the implication of her words. "Well, no. It was utter torture to watch you go out with Jackson—to see you with him at the bonfire."

"Then why on earth are you asking me to—"

Simon squeezed both of her hands once more. "Brianne is your friend. She might know you better than you think. Of course, if you don't want to go, then don't. I'm not going to make you do anything you don't want to." He shrugged. "But admit it. You're a little curious."

He'd expected to see the truth written on her face, plain as day. He'd figured she'd agree with him. Katrina had always been more than a little curious about most things in her life.

But for the first time in his life, she caught him off-guard. With a tone that was not at all humorous, she said, "No."

"No?"

"I'm not curious. I don't need anyone else. I don't want anyone else." She moved into him, forcing him to release her hands so she could wrap her arms around him. Her fingers dug into his back, and she rested her cheek against his chest. "I've been waiting for you to finally say something. I thought for sure you were hiding your feelings." There was a pause and then she chuckled. "I was right."

"Even still..." He pulled away. "Your friendship with Brianne is important, too."

"Then I'll tell her that I realized something tonight and I'm not going to need a date after all. Whoever it is—"

"It's me."

Katrina's mouth snapped shut and her eyes widened. A myriad of emotions flashed behind her eyes. *What?*

"Your date. The guy she wanted to set you up with. It's me." So much for keeping it a secret. Oh well. "You know, it would have been nice to be able to show up with a flower and tell you that Brianne was smarter than both of us. But you being *you*... I didn't want to risk it."

Finally, she reacted. Katrina gasped and whacked his arm. "You're such a jerk. You were going to make me stress about how you felt about me going on a date with someone else, weren't you?" While her tone was accusatory, there was a smile in her eyes. "And then you were going to show up all cocky and everything. I can't believe you!" She let out a sharp laugh. "You're so lucky that I'm in a good mood."

Simon made a show of rubbing his arm, but he wasn't getting any sympathy. He abandoned that move and chuckled, pulling her close again. "Honestly, I don't think Brianne would be able to keep it a secret, anyway. How much you wanna bet that she spilled everything in that message she left you?"

Katrina considered his words. "I don't know. I have a hard time believing she'd be on board with any of this. If I had to guess, I would say that she's warning me to stay far, far away from you."

That did sound more like the Brianne he knew, but the way she'd pushed him toward Katrina felt a little different. Sure, she might have been doing it just to prove a point. They might not be good together.

He refused to let any of that hold him back. He gazed down at the woman he'd watched and supported over the last couple of decades, still in disbelief that he had finally gotten what he'd always wanted. His life was complete.

She gave him a funny look, tilting her head. "What's that look for?"

He shook his head.

"No, you have to tell me now. Consider it payment for all that stress you would have let me go through just so you could be on the better end of the surprise."

If he wasn't so happy, he might have noticed the way his jaw ached from the smile he still sported. Instead, he noted that Katrina seemed just as happy as he was. "I'm just glad it all worked out. I'm the luckiest guy in the world." He pulled back, his eyes sweeping over her wardrobe and one brow lifted. "I thought you said you were getting ready for bed. Sorry, but your jeans and this shirt beg to differ." He reached out to touch the collar of her shirt and Katrina swatted him away.

"Just be glad I'm not dressed in sweats. I bet you wouldn't have been so interested in confessing your love for me if I was dressed how I used to be when I first got back to town." Her voice was lighthearted, free from the angst that had weighed her down for so long.

But it wasn't how she'd said it that threw him off guard.

It was what she'd said.

He hadn't told her he loved her.

Had he?

Simon ran through their conversation in his head, unable to remember if he'd said he loved her or if he had confessed that he simply wanted to see where this could go. His delayed reaction caught her attention and she frowned, inching closer.

"What's the matter?"

He blinked, reminding himself to smile again. "Nothing. I was just thinking."

She slipped her arms around his back and pressed her body into his. The way she fit against him like a missing puzzle piece had him thinking even harder about what she'd said.

He did love her and he knew it. But was it the kind of love she was talking about? It had to be. At this point, her mistake might simply be God's way of helping him know exactly where they both fit.

Simon's arms tightened around her and he rested his chin on top of her head.

This was exactly where he was meant to be. They fit together better than peanut butter and jelly.

Rather than heading inside, Katrina and Simon ended up sitting on the porch. He laced his fingers with hers and she rested her cheek against his shoulder. Simon had lost track of time, but that didn't matter, either.

There was nowhere else he would rather be than with Katrina by his side.

The door to the house opened behind them. There was no pulling away, no jumping apart to hide what had started between them. Instead, Katrina glanced over her shoulder. She turned back just as quickly. "Oh, hi, Daniel."

Daniel glanced between Simon and Katrina, grinning like he'd just walked in on something inappropriate.

"Isn't it a little late for you to be up?" Katrina teased when her brother didn't speak immediately.

"Isn't it a little late for you to be out here with a guy?"

She snuggled more against Simon. "I'm sure your wife is waiting for you somewhere. You probably should hurry home."

Daniel moved past them, heading down the steps, then stopped and faced them. His eyes appraised Simon, then Katrina. When he brought back his focus to Simon, he nodded. "Do you need to reschedule our meeting in the morning?"

The grin he sported said everything his words couldn't. This was his baby sister and he wanted nothing more than to tease her.

Katrina must not have noticed because she jumped, her head swiveling around to stare at Simon. "You finally called him?"

"Called? Nah. Your brother practically ambushed me."

She shot a confused look toward Daniel, who shrugged.

"But yeah," Simon confirmed. "We're going to meet over coffee so he can give me some pointers on starting a new business."

Her hand tightened on his. "I'm so glad to hear it." She brought his hand to her lips, kissing it before she got to her feet and pulled him up with her. "If you're going to get coffee in the morning, you should probably get to bed." Her face drew nearer to his and her voice lowered. "I'll come by your place when you're done, okay?"

"Sheesh, you two. Get a room already," Daniel muttered, his fun having been spent.

Simon chuckled. He brushed Katrina's hair from her face and pressed a lingering kiss to her lips. "I'll see you tomorrow."

CHAPTER THIRTEEN

Katrina had thought she couldn't have been happier when she'd gotten her job in New York. Then when she'd moved to LA. Coming home had been like experiencing a death in the family, but it wasn't a person she'd mourned —it was her career.

There was still a hole in her heart, longing for what might have been, and she wasn't prepared to give up on that dream just yet. But for now, she was going to see where this thing with Simon would go.

She wasn't an idiot. She knew they were still two very different people with two very different ideas of what they wanted out of life, but that didn't mean they couldn't find a way to make it work.

If she ended up finding a job that she was happy with, they would cross that bridge when they came to it.

This new change in her life created a fresh zest that had her looking at everything differently. The sky was brighter, the lavender scent in the fields was sweeter. Life in general seemed more fulfilling than before.

And all because she'd found the connection she'd been craving.

Katrina got up early on Saturday morning to help Bo with the chores. She didn't make one complaint and found it humorous when she overheard her brothers talking about the fact that something had gotten into her.

Apparently, Daniel hadn't had a chance to spill the beans to Bo, Andrew, or Jack. They'd find out eventually. For now, she fully intended on sharing her news with only one other person.

She pulled up in front of Brianne's house at barely past seven. Brianne probably wasn't even out of bed yet. They'd had a late night and she wasn't born and raised on a ranch.

Luckily, she didn't live with her family either, so Katrina could pound on her door all morning long.

Her fist connected with the wooden barrier several times before the door swung open and a bleary-eyed Brianne glowered at her. "What are you doing? Do you even know what time it is?" she demanded.

Katrina pushed past her, holding up the two coffee cups she'd grabbed on her way over. "I got coffee."

Brianne's place was on the small side, and no amount of open concept was enough to make it feel bigger. The kitchen had a total of six cupboards, a single sink, and it was void of a dishwasher. But Brianne could afford it and she liked to be on her own, so this was where they hung out when Katrina got tired of her family.

"So? I didn't get to bed until four hours ago."

Katrina whirled around and stared at her friend. "What are you talking about? You left before Simon did."

At the mere mention of Simon's name, Brianne reacted. He was right. She wouldn't be able to hide the fact that she knew something. That much was certain.

Moving across the room, Katrina pushed the hot cup at her friend. "Tell me you didn't stay up all night talking on the phone to Jackson's friend."

Another chagrined look.

"Brianne! You said you have to leave some mystery. What happened to making sure they want to keep coming back?"

"Well, you certainly have that with Jackson. I don't know what you did to him, but he keeps pestering us to go on another double."

Katrina lifted one brow, taking a sip of her drink. She waited for a moment before speaking. "Us?"

"Yeah, his friend. He wanted us to all do something tonight."

This was it. This would be the moment when Brianne would have to tell her. Based on the vague message last night, Katrina hadn't been entirely sure that Brianne would spill Simon's secret. This morning, she had a better idea of what might be discussed.

Now, she needed to hear it from her friend's own lips. "You didn't tell him that I was available, did you? I got your message—the one about going out tonight. Tell me you didn't agree to give Jackson one more chance."

Brianne took a gulp of her drink and winced, then shot Katrina a dark look. "Of course not. I wouldn't do that to you."

"Good. Because I really don't want to have to see him again."

"What's so wrong with him?" Brianne moved across her small living room and settled onto the love seat. She curled her legs beneath her, pulling her robe tighter around her. "Seriously, Katrina. I don't get why you don't like the guy. He's actually trying. That's a lot more than other guys would do. I'd say that's a sign that you shouldn't be tossing him aside."

She stared hard at her cup, prompting Katrina to take a seat beside her.

"There's nothing wrong with him. He just turned me off when he said my career choice was a joke."

"To be fair, he said it sounded like a hard market and you should settle for something else."

"Exactly," Katrina muttered. "Simon never did that."

Brianne jumped, launching a pointed finger at her friend. "Ha! I knew there was something going on between you two. I just can't believe I didn't see it before."

Katrina rolled her eyes. "Simon already told me about the date tonight."

Brianne's mouth fell open. "What?"

"Yeah, he came over last night." This time, Katrina's smile stole across her face, and it was all she could do to contain her giggle.

"He did?"

"Yeah." She bit down on her lower lip, wishing she knew exactly what Brianne was thinking in this moment. She didn't know if her friend was on board, which made it incredibly difficult to have this little girl-talk go the way she wanted.

Brianne's expression was void of any emotion. No irritation, but also no excitement. She'd wanted this—well, not this specifically, but she'd wanted Katrina to find someone who could take her mind off everything that was going on with her job.

Her friend glanced at her and let out a sigh. "Are you sure this is what you want?"

"Most definitely."

She sighed again. "You can't know that for sure. What if it fails?"

Katrina shrugged. "Simon and I are adults. It doesn't have to be messy. We would just go our separate ways."

Brianne didn't look convinced. She frowned, looking off at something across the room. "I don't know that I can agree with that sentiment. You don't know what he said last night."

The flutters in her chest returned with a vengeance. Goosebumps erupted all over her body. "*You* don't know what he said to me last night."

"Yeah? How about you tell me." Brianne's flat voice didn't instill the kind of encouragement Katrina was looking for.

The wind left her sails just like that and she slumped against the love seat. "If you don't think this is a good idea, then why did you tell him to go out with me tonight?"

"I never said I didn't think it would work out. I said I'm not sure you will be able to maintain your friendship based on what I saw last night and what I'm seeing right now. You two are already so close. You're bound to get closer."

"That's sorta the point."

"Yeah, but when something doesn't work, you guys are going to get in a fight, and in the end, feelings will be hurt."

Katrina snorted but her outward reaction was the complete opposite of the unease that had started creeping in. "We're best friends, Brianne. We're not going to get in a fight because we already know how to communicate better than most new couples. We have the upper hand."

"And what if you end up finding a job out of state? You think he's going to be on board with that?"

She looked away. "I've already thought about that. Either he comes with me, or he doesn't. But that doesn't mean that we have to fight. We can go our separate ways on good terms." When she glanced back toward her friend, she already knew what to expect.

Brianne's look of disbelief was nothing compared to the tendrils of concern she already felt.

No. She wasn't going to let Brianne's pessimistic view of things drag her down.

Not today.

Katrina swallowed back the worry and sat upright. "This is Simon. He's been around forever. He knows that I want that job. He knows what I would do if I got it."

"And what if he wants you to stay here?"

She huffed. "That would never happen. He respects me too much. Besides, he keeps telling me he just wants me to be happy. He's the perfect guy."

"There is no such thing," Brianne murmured.

"Are you going to celebrate with me? Or am I going to have to shove all my joy down your throat before I leave?"

There was an edge to her voice she hadn't expected to come through. Clearly, Brianne heard it as well and it caught her off guard.

The smile she forced on her face couldn't have been more obviously done to placate Katrina, which seemed to put an even bigger damper on the conversation. Still, she played her part as best friend the exact way she needed to. "You're right. Of course, you're right. Tell me everything."

Katrina eyed Brianne for a moment, then took a deep breath to soothe every thought of discontent that had materialized. She allowed herself to feel the joy from the night before at full power and grinned. "He came over and demanded to see me…"

Throughout the whole story, she watched her friend carefully. Brianne made all the right comments. She played her role just as well as could be expected given her obvious disdain for the relationship Katrina was developing.

They steered clear of her job hunt and Katrina asked Brianne about the guy she was spending time with.

"Kurt is the sweetest. But he's not from around here." Brianne took a sip of her drink, the usual shine returning to her eyes as she spilled the information she had on the guy she liked.

"That shouldn't matter. He lives by Jackson, right?"

Brianne shook her head. "Actually, he lives in Texas."

Katrina sucked in sharply. "You're joking. How did I not know that?"

"Well, did Jackson talk about him?"

She shook her head. "He talked mostly about himself—well, until he realized that I wasn't interested in just hearing about him. Then he tried to get to know me better."

"Are you one hundred percent sure you don't just—"

Katrina held up a hand. "I'm going to stop you right there. Simon has been there for me longer than anyone. We've been friends since before you and I were friends. If a relationship with anyone can work, it will be between us."

WHEN YOU'RE FINALLY HOME

She'd repeat those words until she was blue in the face because her happiness depended on it.

And being with Simon made her happy.

Brianne leaned over and touched Katrina's knee. "Then I'm glad it's working out." Her eyes turned serious—so much so that Katrina shivered. "And if he ever hurts you, then I know where some heavy machinery is and there's a lot out back behind my mom's jewelry store where we can bury the body."

Katrina gasped then laughed out loud. "Brianne! He's your friend, too!"

"Yeah, but you're my best friend and I'm not going to let anything happen to you."

She leaned forward and gave Brianne a tight hug. "I don't know how I got to be so lucky to find two people who care about me as much as you guys do."

Brianne pulled back first and wiped at a tear Katrina hadn't realized had slipped down her cheek. "I know, right? You're pretty darn lucky."

Katrina laughed.

"But in all seriousness, you know we love you, right? We'd do anything for you."

"And I'd do anything for you guys."

Brianne nodded. "We know."

CHAPTER FOURTEEN

Simon had been on this porch step more times than he could count. He'd lost track of how many times he'd sat here and let Katrina cry over something devastating, or how often he'd celebrated with her over a win.

This front porch step was as much his home as it was hers. When she'd left town for college, he'd even missed coming here to the point that he'd paid her family a couple of awkward visits just so he could run his hand along the smooth, wooden rail.

Now he was standing on this bottom step with a very different plan in mind.

He was finally going to take Katrina out on a date.

This exact moment would be etched into his brain for as long as he was alive. His heart pounded, his pulse soared, and his stomach knotted so tight he wasn't sure he could even eat.

Simon swallowed back his nerves and took the six steps two at a time. He got onto the porch and lifted his hand to knock, only for the door to swing open before he made contact.

His lungs stopped working in that exact moment, leaving him without even a breath of oxygen.

Katrina wore a simple dress, a blue number that came to her knees. Her shoulders were bare except for two small straps. The neckline came down into a 'v,' drawing his eyes up toward her face.

She blushed prettily, her hand coming up to the hair that was draped over her shoulder. "Hi, Simon," she whispered.

All at once, it was like the wind came back to his chest, nearly knocking him to his feet. "You look…" He shook his head. There were no words to describe the beauty of the woman who stood in front of him. There never had been.

He reached forward and took her hand in his to pull her against him. "I can't believe it's finally happening."

She laughed. "I can't believe it, either. I feel like we've lost so much time because we didn't figure this out sooner."

Simon shook his head. "None of that. No regrets. Tonight is about us." He brought her hand to his lips and brushed a kiss to her knuckles. "Tonight, I fully intend on showing you just how important you are to me."

The smile on her face made all the waiting totally worth it.

He tugged her down the steps to his truck. He opened her door, guided her into the truck, and shut the door firmly. His hands shook. They'd never done that before—not when he'd applied for his first job, not when he'd gone on his first date. Not even with his first high school kiss.

If anything told him this was something that would last a lifetime, it was how his body reacted to her.

Simon took a moment to compose himself before opening his own door. He sucked in a deep breath and released it slowly. Then he climbed in beside her. "What did Brianne have to say about tonight?"

"Brianne?"

He chuckled. "You can't keep stuff like this from her. I know you, Katrina."

She grinned, looking out her window. Her hands were clasped in her lap, and he reached for the one closest to him. Katrina glanced down at their hands and then back to him. "She said she's worried."

He frowned. That wasn't what he wanted to hear.

"But she also thinks that if anyone can do this, then it's us."

That was a little better.

"Well, I don't think she has anything to worry about. I've finally got you and I'm not letting you go."

Katrina scooted a little closer to him. Placing her free hand against his cheek, she smiled. "I think you're completely right. I can't think of a single couple with more history than us. We're gonna be the ones that set everyone straight."

He leaned closer and kissed her, deeply, passionately, and with a promise that everything was going to work out.

∼

THE RESTAURANT HUMMED with quiet chatter. Simon had been here with Katrina a hundred times before, but in none of those experiences was he her date.

He sat across from her in a dimly lit corner booth of the Steer House and watched her read through the menu as if it was the first time he'd ever seen her before. Katrina Reese was on a date with him tonight—no one else.

She glanced up over the edge of her menu and laughed. "What?"

"I just can't believe we're here—together—like this."

Katrina put her menu down and picked up her glass of water. "Well, you'd better start believing it. We're gonna have a lot of questions coming our way once people start noticing the way you're looking at me. You're gonna have to make sure you get your story straight so *they* believe it, too."

He grasped her hand in his. "I think this will help."

She laughed.

"I love it when you laugh."

"You sound so cheesy! We've been here before. We've spent countless hours together here."

"Yeah," he looked down at her hand thoughtfully, rubbing his thumb along the ridges of her knuckles, "but this is different."

She didn't respond right away. When he finally got the nerve to look up at her, she nodded with a whisper. "Yeah, not like this."

"What can I get you folks?" Lacey came up beside their table, and it took all of one second for her eyes to land on their intertwined hands before darting to meet Katrina's. "Well, it's about time!"

Katrina straightened, glancing over to Simon with confusion.

Lacey chuckled. "Oh, you guys didn't know? The town has been waiting for the two of you to finally figure things out since you were teenagers." She lowered closer to the table and murmured, "You get a lot of the gossip when you see so many people come in and out of the most popular restaurant in town." Lacey pulled herself up straight and winked at Simon. "Good for you."

His smile was strained at best. He couldn't help but wonder how he hadn't heard any of this before. He could believe it, that wasn't the issue. He just wondered why no one had pushed him into this situation before now.

Brianne—his own friend—had had to be the one to do the deed, and somehow, that didn't sit right with him. Everyone else could see something he hadn't. What did it say about him that he had missed this?

Katrina squeezed his hand and he glanced up with a jerk. "Did you want something other than water?"

Simon shook his head with a smile. "Nope. Water's good."

The moment Lacey left, Katrina leaned forward. "Are you okay?"

His brows furrowed. "Do you ever feel like you should have been able to see this a long time ago—like the rest of the town, apparently?"

She squeezed his hand once more, and he was surprised at just how soothing it could be. "I think we were different people back then. We didn't need each other that way."

"But now we do."

Katrina tilted her head and her eyes narrowed slightly. "You know something? I don't think we need each other that way even now. I just think we've realized that we want to be together."

She couldn't be more right. This was one of the reasons he cared about her the way he did. Katrina could see things in a way that just made more sense.

Before he had a chance to tell her that, she leaned forward. "You know what else?"

He leaned forward too, as if the two of them were conspiring. "What?"

"I think we should be somewhere else tonight."

He frowned. "What do you mean?"

"I mean maybe tonight we should just do something different. Something that might start a new thing for us."

"Like what?"

Katrina cocked her head, her focus shifting to their hands. She traced lines along his skin with her thumb and her eyes brightened as she lifted them to meet his. "I know exactly where we should go."

"Okay. I'm in. I trust you."

"Well, you should because this is going to be good."

She grabbed her purse and pulled out a ten dollar bill and placed it on the table.

Simon frowned. "You're not supposed to pay for anything. It's a date. Remember?"

Katrina got out of the booth and held her hand out to him. "We have lots more dates for you to make up for a ten dollar tip I left for Lacey. Let's go."

Simon chuckled and stood up as he took her hand. "Good point."

Once they were in Simon's truck, Katrina shared her plan. "We're going to stop to pick up a few snacks and then we're going to your place. We'll sit outside and enjoy the fresh air. What do you think about that?"

"It sounds like the perfect plan."

As they passed beneath the streetlights as they drove through town, he was able to catch glimpses of the grin he adored so much. If someone had told him when he was sixteen that he'd end up winning this girl over, he would have laughed in their face. Katrina had always been the girl he was never going to get. And now here she was, in his truck, holding his hand.

Simon brought her hand to his cheek and turned his lips to kiss her palm. "Yeah, it's the perfect plan."

"I thought you'd like it."

They pulled up to the edge of the huge front yard of her family's property and Simon cut the engine. He got out and pulled the bags of food from the back and grabbed the blanket he always kept for emergencies in the winter.

They settled onto the blanket as they pulled the snacks out and started to nibble. The sun was just about to set and everything about this setting was perfect. Simon couldn't think of anywhere he'd rather be and he certainly wouldn't want to be with anyone but Katrina. But there was the part of him that worried Katrina might look back on this night with regret. Expectations had been high and this was a very low key first date.

"So I love your idea—you know being out here where we grew up is comfortable. It's where we started out. But... I don't know... are you sure you won't think back on our first date and wish we'd done something more exciting?" He hated to start things off on a negative note, but he couldn't let go of this one worry.

"Don't be silly. This was my idea, and I just want to be with you. Doesn't it make sense to spend tonight just the two of us in the place we know the best?" She shrugged and then smiled. "It makes sense to me."

"You've lived on both coasts and small town Rocky Ridge doesn't offer what a big city does. I just don't want you to be disappointed."

"Aww, Simon. I don't expect big city life here. I won't lie and say I don't love the city. I do. But here is home. With you." She reached for his hand and took a grape and fed it to him. "And besides… we'll have plenty of time to enjoy the Steer House. And you can take me to The Aviary. That's plenty high class for me."

"You make good points. And of course I'm happy that there might be a second date after tonight." Simon's laugh peeled out into the night as he scooted a little closer to her.

Her lips quirked upward. "If it makes it any better for you, I might allow you to make this simple date worth my while."

Her soft voice hummed along all his nerve endings. How many times had he wished something like this would happen to him? How often had he lain awake at night wondering if he'd ever get a shot with her?

Well, now he had it and he wasn't willing to mess it up.

"Fine. I think I can take that task on."

His pulse exploded. There was no holding back. His heart was completely done for. Simon grasped her chin, stealing the kiss he'd been anxious to take since he'd picked her up earlier in the evening. She tasted better than he could have ever imagined—sweet and tantalizing with a hint of something he couldn't put his finger on.

Katrina was the girl he knew he wanted to marry.

There, he'd finally admitted it to himself. Simon was finally one step closer to getting everything he ever wanted, and it all started with Katrina losing that job.

What they said was true. When one door closed, a window would always open.

That was what happened with them, and he hoped one day they could look back at this moment and appreciate it for what it was—the start of a beautiful future where anything could happen.

Now, he just needed to help her see just how great staying in Rocky Ridge could be.

And he had the perfect idea.

CHAPTER FIFTEEN

THREE WEEKS LATER

"Okay, you can open your eyes now."

Katrina grinned, her hands still covering her eyes as Simon's voice floated around her. "I know where we are. You get that, right? I don't think there's anything you can do to surprise me."

With that, she lowered her hands and glanced around.

Exactly as she'd expected. She was at Simon's new home.

She gave him a pointed look. "All I see is a dated living room. And let me guess…" She motioned toward a door that was far too skinny to be anything but the entrance to a kitchen that was built at least fifty years ago. "That's the kitchen."

As many times as she'd come to visit Simon at his new farm, she'd never entered the house. Simon had told her he wasn't ready for her to see just how bad it was. Her gaze swept through the room that still had that terrible shag carpet from a time before she was born. The walls were covered in wallpaper that wasn't necessarily terrible—it just felt busy.

The focal point of the room had to be the fireplace, but even it looked in desperate need of an upgrade.

"What exactly am I looking at?"

Simon gestured with both hands to their surroundings. "Have fun."

What was that supposed to mean? There was a built-in bookshelf in one corner of the space, but she doubted there were any books she'd want to read. "Thanks, but I didn't come here to hang out in your terrible living room. I came here to spend time with you. What are we going to do today? Is there anything you need help with out in the barn?"

He chuckled as he moved toward her and slipped his hands around her waist. "No, I want you to decorate it for me."

This time, she didn't know how to react. Her eyes grew wide, and she stared at the room with fresh eyes. "You want me to decorate it?"

Simon brushed a soft kiss to the tip of her nose. "I want you to do what you do best. I want you to tear out the carpet, replace the wallpaper, pick out furniture…"

"Simon," she murmured breathlessly, "that's going to cost a fortune. Never mind me withholding a fee, all the materials you'd need would just be… too much."

He grinned as if he had a secret he had been holding onto until this very moment.

"What?" she demanded. "What are you keeping from me?"

"Everything was finalized with the lawyers regarding Mr. Gregory's estate. He had a life insurance policy, too. And I guess he put my name on it because he wanted me to run the place."

"What? Why?"

Simon shrugged, his eyes bright as ever. "What would you do if you knew the person who was taking over the one thing you loved couldn't do so without financial assistance?"

"Wow," she whispered, looking around the room with fresh eyes. "And you want to spend some of it on updating your home? Wouldn't you prefer to invest that money into the company side of things? I mean, it'd be neat to see this place updated, but—"

His hold on her tightened, causing her heart to bounce around like it had no will of its own. "This place is going to be my home for a very long time. I'd like it to feel as such." His smile widened. "And there's no one better to see that vision through than the one person who has been with me since the beginning. You have the talent and the know-how. You're perfect for the job."

She gasped, finally accepting what he was trying to give her. This was a gift—a way for her to get back on her feet and gain the confidence she needed to get back out there.

No one but Simon would have thought to do this for her, and that was why she only had one answer. "Of course I'll do it." Katrina placed both hands on either side of his face and pressed a firm, unyielding kiss to his lips.

Never had anyone given her something so meaningful. If there was any proof that she was headed down the right path, it was this moment, right here.

And she couldn't wait to get started.

~

While Simon worked the fields and cared for the dairy cows, Katrina busied herself with the smaller tasks like tearing down the wallpaper and pulling up the carpet. She wanted to start on the primary suite, but Simon had insisted on fixing up the common areas first. They were the rooms that would be visited more often by guests.

She couldn't say she agreed with his way of thinking. To her, the room where he would be spending most of *his* time should be given priority.

As far as a bigger picture was concerned, it didn't really matter which room she fixed up first just so long as she got to all of them before she found her dream job in the city. It was like Simon had said. He planned on living here for the long haul. That meant she had plenty of time.

Even if she got a job offer elsewhere, she would surely be coming back here regularly.

And at this point, she wasn't even sure a new job was going to happen, so she'd convinced herself not to expect anything good *or* bad. She wanted to live in the here and now, which was something she'd struggled with since coming back to town.

Katrina dumped some of the light gray paint into a tray and pushed her roller through it before she pressed it against the wall. She hummed a little tune as she worked, loving even the more hands-on aspect of designing Simon's place.

There was a knock on the open door and she glanced over her shoulder to find Daniel. He poked his head inside and let out a whistle. "This place is actually looking a lot better."

She stepped back, hand on her hip, and admired her work so far. "It is, isn't it?"

"What do you have planned?"

Motioning toward one side of the room, she waved a hand through the air. "How about a bay window?"

Daniel snorted.

"What?" she demanded.

"If you want to knock out this wall and put in a bay window, you really shouldn't be painting it."

She gave her brother a flat look. "I'm painting it because he wants it to be livable. Simon wants to entertain people here in the next several months or years. And he deserves to have a space where he can invite friends without them making fun of his wallpaper and carpet."

Daniel shot a look toward the floor and before he could ask her, she gave him the details.

"Simon wants wood floor in here. He'd like it to go to the kitchen through here." Katrina took a few steps toward the doorway she'd had a local handyman expand. "It's not going to be open concept, but it'll be so much better after I'm through with it."

Her brother appraised her, nodding. "I don't doubt it." With one more sweep through the living room, he let his eyes focus on Katrina. "And what if you get offered one of those jobs you were so interested in? What then?"

"What do you mean? I'm going to take the job."

Daniel's brows drew together. If she didn't know any better, she might have thought he was judging her.

"I'm not just going to abandon what I want because some guy told me I'm pretty."

"That *some guy* deserves to know where you stand and what your plans are. Does he even know that you don't want to stick around?"

"Of course he knows. Everyone knows. It's not like I kept it a secret. I've always wanted to work for a bigger firm in the city. I just don't fit in around here."

"Have you even tried?"

She shot him a sharp look. How dare he question her and the things that made her happy? He wasn't her father. And he certainly hadn't cared before now. What had gotten into him?

"*Yes*, I've tried. Besides with our family and Simon, I don't really belong anywhere and I feel like whatever is out there waiting for me has to do with my future in design."

She could see the disappointment in his eyes. Or *was* it disappointment? Either way, her brother wasn't pleased with her plans. "What's it to you, anyway?"

"We care about Simon, too. And I, for one, don't want to see him lose something he clearly cares about."

"No one said he'd *lose* me."

Daniel shook his head with a sigh. "Whatever. Look, I came by to talk to him about something. Do you know where he is?"

She flicked her fingers in the general direction of the barn. "You guys are all alike. One of these days, you're going to realize that work isn't everything."

"Speak for yourself," Daniel muttered. "The pot needs to stop calling the kettle black if you ask me."

Katrina would have demanded he take it back, but he was long gone.

And he was wrong.

She didn't prioritize her career over her relationships. She'd kept up on the friendships she'd had while she was working in the city before. It wouldn't be any different if she left again.

Simon might love this farm, but he wasn't married to it. He could be persuaded to leave it and start a life with her in the city if that was where their relationship ended up.

While she tried to convince herself that everything would be okay, she lost the oomph she'd had only moments ago when she'd been excited about the new paint.

What if she was wrong?

No.

She refused to let herself believe that. Simon was far too close of a friend, and now a boyfriend, for her to assume he would do anything to hurt her, and that included keeping her from chasing after her dreams.

Katrina needed to get her head on straight and actually do what she'd come here for—to make sure Simon's home was something he could take pride in. And at the same time, she would take pride in the thing that gave her joy—design.

Simon was aware of this. That was why he'd offered to let her have at it. And this was why they worked out so well together. Daniel didn't know what he was talking about.

The longer she ruminated on these points, the more she realized that she needed to get back to her job hunt. Ever since she'd allowed her friends to get her out of the house and busy on other things, she'd let her applications lapse. She wasn't even sure if any of them were viable anymore.

Katrina would have to submit a few new resumés and see what was out there.

There was a small niggling doubt that wriggled into her head over what her brother had said, but she pushed it aside. If Simon cared about her like she knew he did, he would understand this was simply part of who she was.

As soon as she got home, she would submit a few new applications to places. Perhaps she'd even check out some businesses that were closer. It wouldn't be the end of the world if she had to move to Billings. Sure, it was a couple hours away, but that was better than having to move all the way to New York like before.

Her mood slowly improved as she continued to work. Everything was falling into place in her mind, and she couldn't wait to tell Simon all about it. However, she wasn't going to get her hopes up. She could wait until she had an actual offer. That would be better. Then they could have something to celebrate together.

The remainder of her afternoon went a little better than she'd expected. With a new surge of energy, Katrina was able to finish her painting and touch up the baseboards. In three days, the new flooring would arrive and she could call the room complete.

Normally, Simon was done with his work before she was, but today was different. It probably had something to do with what Daniel wanted with him. Rather than go track him down, Katrina moved through the house to pick out her next project. She wandered down the hall and ended up at Simon's bedroom door.

While she should wait for his permission to enter his space of solitude, she couldn't help herself. The door was already a crack open and all it took was a nudge to push it all the way.

She poked her head inside and stared, stunned, at how clean and organized it was. But then again, this was Simon and he wasn't the typical guy. She'd been raised with four brothers and none of them were as good at keeping a place tidy as Simon.

One foot after the other, she found herself standing just inside the room. The space wasn't bad. Even the hardwood floor didn't seem to fit the rest of the house. Either Simon had been holding out on her and he'd done some work without her knowing, or he didn't want to disappoint her with a project that wasn't on the larger scale.

Katrina didn't dare move farther into the room in case Simon returned from his work. Instead, she made a mental note of the color schemes and anything small she could do to breathe new life into this bedroom without a major overhaul.

A smile stole across her face. She could surprise him with that, too. It would be her way of saying thank you for everything he'd done for her over the years.

CHAPTER SIXTEEN

Over the next week, Simon wasn't able to spend nearly as much time with Katrina as he wanted to. While she continued fixing up his place by working her magic, he had finally gotten to a point where he could see his dream business come to fruition.

With help from Daniel and his wife's financial connections from her work in New York, along with the money he'd received in the inheritance, Simon could finally put everything into motion.

The dairy farm would continue. He was in a place where he could make that work. But he was going to focus on horse training, too. He knew he'd need plenty of help, but that wasn't a worry.

He'd kept his plans secret from Katrina, not because he didn't think he'd be able to make it work, but because he knew what it might do to her emotionally. Even though Katrina seemed happier lately, he couldn't shake the feeling that she was settling somehow. There was a very real possibility that she would tire of Rocky Ridge. If she got to the point where she felt trapped, it wouldn't take much for her to go off in search of something better—well, better in her opinion.

As much as he hated to admit it to himself, he was still worried he wasn't enough for her. But that was how Katrina had always been. She'd always had big dreams and he might not be the one to help her create the life she wanted.

Simon found himself spending some of his spare time in the barn as he contemplated what might happen next. Of course, he couldn't run from it. Eventually, he'd have to talk to her about where he wanted their future to be—together.

He simply wasn't ready for that yet. He wanted to enjoy the life they were currently living. It had been nearly two months since they'd started this dance and she hadn't brought up her job or what she wanted to do now that she'd settled in.

Katrina was still helping out at her family's ranch, but not enough to make Simon believe that it was what she wanted. Her working on his place was the first time he'd seen the spark return in a long time.

Was he delaying the inevitable?

Most definitely.

At least he didn't have wool pulled over his eyes. They'd figure it out. He had to believe that.

Tonight, he was just taking some quiet time so he could revel in what he had accomplished. He was also waiting for Daniel and Megan to show. Simon had made an executive decision to hire Megan to help him get everything up and going, and now all he had left was to cross the t's and dot the i's.

Perhaps tonight was the night he would tell Katrina his plans for the future. Then he could make sure she was aware just how big of a part he wanted her to play in that future.

Even the thought of confirming what she probably already knew was enough to get his heart racing. This wasn't a proposal. He didn't have a ring, and he wasn't asking her to move in with him. But he was telling her that he had no intention of dating anyone else and he wanted her to know she was it for him.

His whole body was on edge, mentally and physically. All the steps he planned to take over the next couple of months were going to change both of their lives forever.

"Simon? You in here?" Daniel poked his head in the doorway. Evening had fallen behind him and the glow from the barn light illuminated only his face to make it appear he was floating. Behind Daniel, Megan materialized.

Simon still couldn't get past the way Megan looked like she'd just walked out of a corporate office. She'd been living here for long enough, he would have thought her wardrobe would have changed to match. But then if she stopped wearing her pantsuits and donned a cowboy hat, he wasn't sure he'd recognize her.

Megan smiled warmly at him and waved a manila folder in the air. "Guess what I have," she sang.

Simon placed his hands on his knees and stood from the bale of hay he'd been sitting on. He moved toward her, and his heart accelerated even faster. At some point, he was bound to have a cardiac event if he didn't get his nerves under control. Holding out his hand, he took the folder and flipped it open.

"I take it the city approved my business registration. And the loan?" He glanced up at Megan, who nodded.

"Better than we expected."

His eyes widened and he turned his focus back to the paperwork until he found the document. "You're kidding," he muttered.

"Nope. Seems when Daniel was willing to co-sign with you, it bumped up your credibility." Megan gave her husband a warm look, the kind that Simon often gave to Katrina. It was nice to see the love these two shared seemed comparable to that he had for Katrina. It made him feel like he had a shot at his own happily ever after.

"I can't believe it. I didn't think it was going to be so easy."

"It's amazing what you can accomplish when you set your mind to something, right?" Daniel chuckled, clapping his hand on Simon's shoulder. "You've earned it. I don't think I've seen anyone work as hard as you did. The research alone would have made my head explode."

Megan slipped her arm around Daniel's waist and leaned into him before resting her cheek against his shoulder. "To be fair, Simon has been dreaming about this for a long time. It wasn't just something that fell into his lap."

Daniel scoffed, shooting a mocked-hurt expression in her direction. "That's not fair at all."

She laughed.

Simon watched them interact and found it hard to believe they'd been such at odds with one another not too long ago. Katrina didn't give him all the details, but she did mention that Daniel had absolutely hated Megan when she'd first shown up.

Now, they were in love.

Daniel glanced over to Simon, probably sensing that he was being watched. "Now that you have the loan approval and the business plan in place, you're all set to break ground on the training center you wanted to build. It's going to take a while to get it constructed, so I wanted to offer some space out at our place if you need to board any horses you might buy."

"I don't think I'll be making that kind of purchase yet. I need to get materials for the training, and I wanted to reach out to some of the locals to offer on-site training until it's up and running."

Megan straightened. "That's a wonderful idea. You'll be able to get a loyal client-base and when you move everything here, you'll have an amazing jumping-off point."

"Have you told Katrina yet?"

Daniel's serious voice wasn't expected and it made Simon do a double-take. He glanced toward Megan briefly as if she would know why her fiancé was suddenly not as lively as before.

"Not yet. And thanks, by the way, for not telling her. I wanted to make sure everything would work out. You know the way she got when she lost out on the job she had. I didn't want to trigger anything." Simon forced a smile, suddenly feeling like he was being judged for keeping this from his girlfriend.

Daniel and Megan exchanged glances. Megan reached out and patted his arm. "Don't worry about it. Tell her when you're ready. It'll be a big change for both of you. And just so you know, this is happening. That paperwork in your hand proves it."

"Congrats, man. I'm glad we could do this together. I can't think of a guy I'd rather work with on something like this." Daniel smiled once more toward his wife. "And Megan can attest to just how hard it is for me to work with someone else on their dream."

"Thanks, guys." Simon tapped the folder on his palm. Daniel was right. Even though he hadn't said anything out loud, and he didn't have to, Simon knew it was time.

Still, just because Simon had come to this conclusion didn't mean he was happy about it. He'd go talk to Katrina right now and make sure she knew what was going on. Then he'd make sure she knew how he felt about their future.

He forced another smile and saw the couple off. Stepping out into the darkness, he glanced toward his house. The lights in the front room were on, and he could see through the window just how nice the living room had turned out. By the looks of it, Katrina had done what she could to arrange the furniture.

WHEN YOU'RE FINALLY HOME

His breath caught in his lungs, and he had to focus on drawing in enough oxygen before he made his way toward the front door. He could do this. They'd successfully avoided any conversation regarding her past and what had brought her home, but now it was time to face the music.

He hoped everything would turn out exactly the way he wanted it to. Why not? She was happy. He was excited. They were good together.

Simon pushed open the door but didn't see Katrina anywhere. He ducked his head farther into the living room. She wasn't there. "Katrina?"

There was a soft *thunk* somewhere in the house, but he couldn't place it.

"Katrina? Where are you?"

"One sec!"

Her muffled voice came from the opposite side of the house. He kicked off his boots and glanced down one last time at the folder he held in his hands before moving in the direction where he thought she might be.

There were more thuds, and shuffling, then a door closed and Katrina materialized around a corner. She was breathing heavily, and a strand of hair had come loose from the messy bun on her head. A smudge of paint was on her cheek, probably from touching up something in the living room. But it was the excited grin on her face that made him pause.

She was absolutely breathtaking. Even in overalls and a white tank top, this woman would always be beautiful to him.

One side of his mouth lifted in a curious smile. "Whatcha doing back there?"

He leaned forward. The only rooms on this side of the house were his bedroom, a bathroom for guests, and an oversized storage closet.

He quirked one brow upward as he brought his eyes to meet hers. "Because I distinctly remember telling you that I didn't want you to do anything to my room."

Just by the way she bit on her lower lip and looked away, he knew what had happened. And he wasn't even upset about it. She was clearly so happy with what she'd done, he couldn't take that away from her.

"Okay, so I may have gone a little crazy…" Katrina laughed. "But I think you're going to love it. And then I have to tell you something." She grabbed onto the hand that wasn't holding the folder and pulled him toward his door. "You have to keep in mind I couldn't do much with your furniture all in here. So I didn't paint it, and I couldn't change the flooring. But I redecorated it to match your… certain… flair."

He chuckled. "Okay, then after that, I want to tell you something."

"Deal." She pushed open his door and swept her arms wide. "What do you think?"

His eyes scanned the room. New bedding, a different chair. An antique dresser and a new armoire. There was a rug on the floor next to his bed so his feet didn't immediately touch the cool wood in the winter months. The color scheme really did seem to highlight that he was a country man who owned horses and cattle.

And it was perfect.

Simon's gaze shifted to Katrina, who was practically bouncing on the balls of her feet. "What do you think?" she repeated.

He slipped an arm around her waist and pulled her into his side before pressing a kiss to her temple. "I think you outdid yourself."

"Really? Because—"

"It's perfect, Katrina. I couldn't have asked for anything better." He turned to face her. "And it only makes what I'm going to say even sweeter."

She opened her mouth, but he cut her off. If he didn't tell her about his new business venture now, he might not ever have the nerve to do so.

"I'm doing it."

Her mouth snapped shut and her brows creased with confusion.

"I got the licensing and the permits. I'm the proud owner of a horse training business."

Katrina's eyes widened and she let out a squeal. "That's amazing! I knew you could do it! How long have you been planning this?"

He laughed. "I'll give you all the details over dinner. But for now..." Simon took her hand in his and brushed his thumb over the back of it. "I wanted to talk about us. I know it seems like everything is still so new, but for me, it's different. I knew from the moment we met that you'd be part of my future."

She tugged on her hand, and mumbled, "Simon—"

"And I know marriage isn't something we're quite ready for, but I needed you to know..."

"Simon, I have to tell you—"

"...that you're it for me. No matter what. I want us to be together. You're a big part of who I am." He lifted his eyes to her face, surprised to find her looking so upset. "What's the—"

"I accepted a job offer."

CHAPTER SEVENTEEN

Her own words echoed in Katrina's head. The silence surrounding them pressed in on her and her legs shook. This wasn't how her announcement was supposed to go. She'd wanted to show him the room and tell him about this amazing job opportunity while assuring him that she had no intention of breaking things off.

Only now, she realized what a stupid decision that had been.

Everything was about to change. She'd just been too blind to see it.

She didn't know what she'd expected might happen. Perhaps there was a small part of her that had anticipated he would be willing to pick up and follow her even though he'd just inherited the farm. It was still so new.

But Simon had proved her wrong.

With his new business venture, there was now a zero percent chance that he would ever leave this place. Not for her, not for anyone. He was officially rooted.

And she felt utterly sick to her stomach. That was why she'd settled onto the edge of his bed.

Simon paced back and forth in front of her. There had been a folder in his hand and now it lay on the floor, having slipped from his grasp. She kept looking at it as if it were the sole reason she was in this mess.

"How could you do this? I thought we had an understanding," Simon muttered.

Her eyes snapped up to stare at him. "How could I do what? Follow my dreams? Do you even hear yourself?" She shot to her feet and placed her hands on her hips. "And what understanding was that? You never told me to stop applying for jobs."

"No," he muttered, "but I didn't think I had to. I figured it made sense that we were both here and both interested." Simon ran a rough hand down his face and groaned. "Where?"

"Where?"

He took a deep breath like it was almost painful for him to do something that should have been second nature. "Yes, where are you taking a job? How far away will you be?"

She looked away.

The sound that came from him next was more of a growl than anything else.

WHEN YOU'RE FINALLY HOME

"It's not that bad," she mumbled. "We can still see each other."

"Based on the way you just reacted, forgive me if I don't have much faith in that statement."

She flinched. His tone wasn't sharp; there was no bite to it. But those words caused her grief regardless. "One of the big companies has recently relocated to Salt Lake City."

"*Utah?*"

Again, Katrina flinched. "That would be the one."

"You realize that's, like, a day's drive, right? How is that any better than when you were living in California?"

"It's *ten hours*, Simon. And if we fly, it's only an hour and a half."

He stopped and stared at her. She could practically feel the judgment pouring off him. She couldn't stand the way he was looking at her; it made her skin itch and her muscles tense. They were supposed to be celebrating and planning how to make things work.

Instead, he was angry and she was defensive.

Katrina stormed through the room and out of the house before he had a chance to tell her his true feelings. She could already hear him arguing with her, insisting she tell that company she couldn't take the job. He'd demand that she stay here because there was more at stake if he were to leave.

Simon would probably point out that losing his farm and his business was a bigger loss than her potential career and happiness.

As if she'd turned on autopilot, Katrina found herself back at her place. She didn't know how she'd made it in one piece. She couldn't even remember driving the whole way home.

Her face was flushed and her stomach was in uproar, threatening to release all of its contents. Katrina barely made it to her room, slamming the door behind her as soon as she crossed the threshold.

Tears streamed down her face. They weren't all sad tears, either. These were hot, angry tears, and they existed for no other reason than she was frustrated Simon had changed.

At some point, he had stopped being the person who supported her with blind adoration.

Katrina slumped down on her bed and sat there, staring at nothing in particular. She couldn't blame him for being angry, which was another reason for her frustration. He deserved to find his happiness too. Hadn't she told him he should chase after that idea he had about horse training?

Clutching at herself, she fell back on her bed and closed her eyes as tight as she could. Stars materialized behind her lids, pulsing in beat with the pounding in her head. She'd never thought she'd be stuck in a position like this.

First of all, she'd never envisioned settling down with a cowboy. She'd always seen herself with a man in a suit—someone who owned his own company and could take her to exotic places. But that was all a fairytale. She could see it now.

Just because she hadn't ended up falling for a city boy didn't mean she wasn't still counting on finding a home in a place like Salt Lake or Los Angeles. Even Simon knew how much she wanted to settle down somewhere similar.

He really shouldn't have been surprised.

The more she mulled over these depressing thoughts, the more racked with guilt she became.

Because she really wanted that job—more than New York, more than Los Angeles.

Her chest heaved with more angry sobs. She couldn't walk away from this opportunity. Deep down, she knew that. It was the chance of a lifetime, and they'd assured her that if she stuck it out with them, she'd have the option of working remotely.

That was the only reason she'd accepted. A few years in Utah and maybe she could return to Rocky Ridge.

To Simon.

The tears continued streaming down her face and she rolled onto her side. Based on how Simon had reacted, she wasn't so sure he would be open-minded enough to agree to something like that. She'd heard it in his voice.

Simon wanted to start a family. He didn't want to make her feel pressured, which in and of itself was sweet, but he really wanted them to work out.

Unfortunately, real life was messy, and nothing ever worked out the way she wanted it to. The way Katrina saw it, she had a couple different paths to choose from.

She could quit the job before she'd even started it and plead for Simon to forgive her for her mistake. She could beg him to give the long-distance thing a try and see if eventually she'd be given the opportunity to work remotely. Or she could cut ties off entirely.

That last one made her so sick to her stomach she had to pull a pillow tight against her body to ground her. Since they were both a little on edge and neither would be willing to make the first move, she'd have time to come up with a plan. And if Simon came to her first, then perhaps she wouldn't have to make the hard choices.

Katrina lost track of time. She'd kept her eyes shut and the next thing she knew, there was light pouring into her bedroom. Static made her hair cling to her face and her bedding, giving her the worst bedraggled appearance she was sure she'd ever had.

She couldn't bring herself to climb out of bed, and seeing as no one came knocking on her door, she might even be lucky enough to hide away for the next twenty-four hours. There was zero energy left in her body. Katrina couldn't even bother to roll off the bed and change out of her overalls.

Instead, she stared at the wall, wishing a solution would materialize. She cared for Simon more than she'd cared for anyone. She might even love him, which was why she hadn't had the strength to break it off then and there in his bedroom.

Love.

It wasn't fair.

How could the universe give her someone like Simon for her entire life, keeping him just at arm's reach? How could it then thrust him into her bubble and allow her to fall for him when she clearly had other plans with her life?

But most of all, how could she sit here both weighed down with guilt and yet too stubborn to make a change? Why couldn't she simply let go of her dream?

Because she'd be settling, that's why.

Not that she'd be settling for Simon. He was amazing.

No, Katrina would be settling for a life she didn't want—one that was filled with the mundane and nothing at all like she'd dreamed she'd have. Wasn't that worth something?

A knock at her door startled her and she shot up in bed. Sharp, pinprick stabs sliced through her skull, and she brought her hand to her head as she muttered, "Yeah?"

She'd expected to see Simon, or even her folks or her brothers. But when the door opened and Brianne entered, she got the strangest feeling of déjà vu.

"Brianne?"

Her friend took one look at her and rushed across the room. "What happened? Did Simon—"

"Simon didn't do anything." Katrina glanced sideways at her. "He's perfect."

"Then why isn't he here making you feel better? What happened?"

Katrina grimaced. "I don't know."

"You don't know what happened? Do you need to see a doctor?"

"No," she muttered. "I know what happened, I just don't know how I got here."

Her friend gave her a confused look and Katrina sighed.

"I got a job offer."

Brianne's face broke into a wide smile. "That's amazing! Which one? Are they going to pay you what you're worth? Please tell me it's close."

Her side-eyed stare was all it took for Brianne to understand everything.

"Oh."

"Yeah," Katrina muttered, rubbing her temples. "And now Simon is mad."

"Of course he is."

"You don't have to rub it in."

Brianne scooted closer. She folded her legs beneath her and let out a heavy breath. "I was afraid something like this might happen."

"What are you talking about? You couldn't have possibly—"

Her friend gave her a flat look. "I know you. And Simon knows you, too. The problem is, I'm a realist and he's an optimist. He probably thought all he had to do was get you to fall in love with him and then you wouldn't want to leave. But I knew better."

Katrina's focus was glued to her friend. How was it that Brianne knew her better than she knew herself? Better than Simon knew her? They were close, but she hadn't thought Brianne was capable of such clear thinking.

She sighed again, and nudged Katrina with her knee. "Look, I knew eventually you'd want to leave again. I figured it would happen, and that was one of the reasons I didn't think Simon was a good fit. That guy was born and bred to live here and run his farm. You just want different things."

"And you didn't ever think there was a chance that something might change? That I could change?"

Brianne shrugged. "I don't know. I guess I think everyone can change if they really want to. But this isn't a character flaw or a weakness. You wanted something, so you went out to get it. You're doing everything you can to keep it. The way I see it, we fight for the things that are most important to us."

That didn't make Katrina feel any better. In fact, it almost made her sound selfish. What did it say about her that she wasn't willing to take a different job in order to maintain the relationship she had with Simon?

Another knock sounded at the door and both of them glanced up to see Simon standing there.

Katrina's heart flipped on its side.

"Can we talk?" he murmured.

Brianne patted Katrina's knee. "I'll be downstairs if you need me." She climbed off the bed and gave Simon a pointed look before she brushed past him and disappeared down the hall.

CHAPTER EIGHTEEN

Simon waited until he could no longer hear Brianne's footsteps. There was no telling what Katrina had said to her, but it was more than likely Brianne was officially Team Katrina.

She fidgeted on her bed, wringing her comforter in her hands and avoiding looking at him directly. Her eyes were red-rimmed and somewhat puffy, and her hair was disheveled.

If he didn't know any better, he might have thought she'd had a worse night than he had.

But he did know better.

Simon hadn't slept at all last night. He was exhausted, and after he'd gotten his daily chores done, he'd come right over. They had a lot to discuss—a lot she wouldn't be thrilled to hear him say.

He didn't dare move farther into her room for fear if he did, he might crumble. Instead, he pulled back his shoulders and crossed his arms. If he could get through this conversation with her in one piece, he might just be able to survive the next few months of heartache.

"I didn't think I'd see you so soon," she mumbled.

"I didn't want you to have to wonder where I stand."

She nodded.

"I don't want you to move to Salt Lake."

Again, she nodded. "I know."

"Then why did you apply there?" He took a deep breath, but it shuddered as he exhaled. "Was I… not enough?"

Simon hated the way his voice trembled, thankful that it didn't break entirely.

"Of course you're enough," she muttered, "it's just that I had this vision of what my life would be like, and it wasn't…"

"It wasn't with me."

There it was. That was the answer he needed before he could move forward.

"That's not it at all." Katrina huffed and shifted on her bed, her eyes clouding over. "And you're not being fair. I've always wanted a job that was bigger than myself. You know that. You supported me through it every chance you got. I'm not the one who changed, it's you."

"You're right," he snapped. "I *have* changed. I know what I want and I'm actually willing to go after it."

She stilled, her mouth snapping shut in the process.

WHEN YOU'RE FINALLY HOME

"I know this might not make sense to you, but I want you. I'm in love with you, Katrina. I want *us*."

Her eyes dropped to her hands and her face flushed.

"There's just one big problem." He waited for her to look at him again before he continued. "I don't think you feel the same way."

This time, she straightened and opened her mouth, clearly ready with a snappy comeback, but he held up his hand to prevent her from saying anything that would only make this moment worse.

"I love you too much to let you settle for me."

"Simon—"

"No. You know as well as I do that you'd never be happy here. You know that eventually you would get that itch to move somewhere else. It's who you are. Heck, it's even one of the things that I adore about you. Katrina, you're one of those people who can chase your dreams without the paralyzing fear that you won't be good enough. You have a talent for seeking out new opportunities where you can shine. And I know you'll never get that here. Rocky Ridge isn't your home."

His gut tightened, roiling uncontrollably. "That's why I came here to tell you that we can't continue seeing each other. Not long distance, not even if you stay."

Emotion burned in the back of his throat, and he had to cough to clear it. No weakness. He couldn't show her how much this was tearing him up inside, because then she might actually stay out of guilt.

Katrina had to make her own choices and follow whatever called to her. That was the only way she'd be happy.

"I want you to be happy," he whispered.

She blinked and a tear slipped from her eyelash down her cheek.

He wore a sad smile, but kept his feet rooted where he stood. "I don't want either one of us to feel like we're settling. I wouldn't be able to live with myself if I knew you resented me for making you stay with me. And I refuse to let you blame yourself for us not working out."

"Simon—" she tried again in a whisper, "I don't know if I can—"

"You *can*," he assured her. "And you're going to be amazing." He gritted his teeth, biting down so hard his jaw ached. No emotion. No weakness. Just pure sacrifice. He wanted to tell her he would always love her. He wanted to drop to his knees and beg for her to stay with him, to build their own happily ever after.

But this was real life.

Simon gave her a firm nod and slipped out of the room before he broke completely. He made it halfway down the stairs when hurried footsteps behind him made him stop cold. To hope it was Katrina chasing him down to tell him he was making a mistake would be unrealistic, and he'd decided last night that he needed to be better at viewing the world through the right lenses.

The shuffling footsteps stopped. He didn't dare turn around, not even when he heard Brianne's quiet voice.

WHEN YOU'RE FINALLY HOME

"I heard what you said in there."

And just like that, his heart shattered.

His hand tightened on the railing at his side. Without facing her, he muttered, "Yeah, well, it had to be said."

"I think it has got to be the most selfless thing you have ever done, and you don't have a single selfish bone in your body."

He couldn't breathe. Her words were only making matters worse. What was he supposed to say? Right now, all he wanted was to be that selfish jerk who made demands, because for once in his life, he wanted something to work out for him.

No parents. No family. Until recently, nothing to call his own. And now he'd lost the love of his life. He certainly felt like the universe owed him *something*.

"Is there something you wanted from me, Brianne? I have to get back to the farm."

For a moment, she didn't say anything. He nearly thought she'd slipped away and left him looking like the idiot he was. Then she finally spoke.

"She doesn't know what she's losing." With that, her footsteps faded away.

Simon glanced over his shoulder, finding the staircase empty. That was probably the first meaningful compliment Brianne had given him.

Slowly, he turned back and headed down the stairs. There would be plenty to distract himself with over the next several months. He would be able to dive into his work and hopefully he'd be able to forget all about the feelings Katrina had awoken within him.

He'd been telling her the truth when he told her that there was no one else. Part of him had already come to terms with this when he'd decided to come speak to her.

Katrina would move on to bigger and better things. She might find a new guy to date or even marry. She'd move up in the company she so desperately wanted to be a part of. And he'd remain the same old Simon.

There wasn't a single doubt in his mind that he would end up alone, and he'd made his peace with it. Once he'd experienced love like he had, he wouldn't be able to settle for anything less.

If he had to spend the rest of his days reliving those small moments, he would.

∽

Simon did exactly as he'd told himself he would.

He buried himself in work.

Paperwork, grunt work, and anything else he could fill his time with that would exhaust him to the point he could pass out on the bed in the spare room. There were now two rooms in his home where he couldn't stand to be for more than a few seconds. Everywhere he looked, all he saw were reminders of Katrina, from the bedding she'd replaced to the paint color she'd chosen.

Yes, it looked nice. More than nice—that woman knew what she was doing when she pulled aspects of a room together. It was no wonder those people in Salt Lake City wanted her. She was good.

But that didn't change the fact that he was absolutely miserable in his own home.

Three weeks had gone by since he'd seen her last.

Three whole weeks and he still couldn't bring himself to sleep in his own bed, never mind go to town and visit any of the businesses they'd gone to together. He had to face it. Katrina was a part of his life whether he liked it or not. But what did he expect when he fell for his best friend?

He longed for the day when he could relive their moments together without the deep, heart-wrenching pain that came with it.

The folks around him treated him differently, too. He'd first noticed it when he went into the grocery store and got a few pitying looks. No one talked about Katrina. No one even breathed a whisper of the city where she now resided.

She'd left, and there was no telling whether she'd come back.

Only one good thing had come out of the way they ended things. They were still amicable. She sent the occasional text message—mostly funny memes or pictures of current projects. Mostly, he ignored them.

And then there was Brianne. She hung around a lot more often than she used to. He couldn't tell if she did so because she didn't have anyone else to spend time with, or if she simply felt bad for him and wanted to make sure he wasn't going to do something stupid like drunk dial their friend.

Today, she'd pulled him out of the house to head to town, insisting that they get a treat at the bakery. But the second they exited the building, she wandered off to talk to a cowboy across the street.

Simon watched with veiled fascination as Brianne flirted with a guy he didn't recognize. She'd reach out and touch his arm, laughing. The guy seemed to enjoy it. Normally, this was when Simon would long for that sort of connection with someone.

Before Katrina, he'd longed to have that connection with *anyone*. Now, all he felt was numb. He didn't need anyone anymore.

He took a bite of his ice cream and wandered to a bench where he could wait for Brianne to finish her flirting. Eventually, she'd either get the guy's number or she'd grow tired of the cat-and-mouse game. Then she'd come tell him all about it.

As long as she didn't talk to him about Katrina, he was fine with her company.

Within minutes, she settled down beside him and sighed. "They just don't make them like they used to."

He grunted and she nudged him.

"Hey, I'm talking to you."

Simon glanced in her direction. "Yeah," he said noncommittally. "They don't make us like they used to."

Brianne laughed. "See? You get it. What happened to cowboys bending over backward to win their lady's hearts?"

"Their ladies decide to move away."

She frowned but didn't comment. He shouldn't have said anything. Now she'd be in a sour mood, too.

"When are you going to just talk about it."

He stiffened.

"Because you know you can, right? Just because I'm her friend too doesn't mean you can't talk about it. I think what she did was really stupid."

"Brianne, don't."

"Seriously," she continued as if she didn't hear him. "She made the biggest mistake of her life. No one is going to love her the way you do."

"I mean it, Brianne. Knock it off."

"If she doesn't wise up, you're not going to be here—"

"I'm not talking about this with you." Simon shot to his feet and strode in the direction of his truck. So much for a nice afternoon out.

CHAPTER NINETEEN

For the first time in Katrina's life, she didn't know what she was doing.

She'd taken the job because that was what she expected of herself. Now, she was sitting in a beautiful corner office of a building that rose over the Salt Lake valley, and for some reason, the whole world felt gray.

It wasn't that beautiful dove gray color that everyone demanded she used in her designs—though that was getting old, too. This gray was that dirty dishwater gray that made her whole world feel muddled like there was a fog surrounding her.

Food was bland and so was everything else.

Katrina stared at her computer screen, hating the way her current design was coming together. She couldn't put her finger on just what was wrong. Had she lost her spark? Where was that magic she couldn't seem to contain within herself?

A sigh burst from her chest, and she pushed away from her desk. Grabbing a stress ball that the company had given her when she arrived, she squeezed it several times as she wandered through her office.

The first few days had been great. It had been a whirlwind of getting settled not only in her office but in her small apartment. Everywhere she looked, she saw buildings. There was no escaping the sounds of the city. At first, she'd welcomed the hum and constant noise. It had felt like returning home to a familiar friend.

But quickly, it had started to grate on her nerves.

There were no rolling hills or the sounds of wildlife. The occasional seagull that she saw in parking lots just didn't cut it.

Maybe she'd made a mistake. She'd jumped at the first offer she'd gotten that was both close and in an area she thought she could enjoy. There was even a lot more to see around here. She could go a half hour in one direction and find herself in the mountains of Park City. She could go in the opposite direction and see all the trees changing colors in the canyons.

Granted, she didn't have a lot of time to just explore. She was still Katrina Reese, and as such, she liked to showcase just how much she was worth to her company.

The people were great, too. She'd already made a little group of friends. She had two roommates, and three coworkers who had taken her under their wings.

If the area and the people weren't the problem, there was only one reason why she didn't feel like she belonged.

Simon.

As much as she hated to admit it, this place didn't quite measure up to what she'd anticipated. All her life, she'd wanted to be in the big city. She'd thought small towns were just too tiny and insignificant.

Boy, did she feel wrong.

But there was no going back. She couldn't just pick up and head home with her tail between her legs. Even if she could and not destroy her reputation, there was a zero percent chance that Simon would forgive her and take her back.

And that was the worst part.

"That Colbert case is a tricky one, isn't it?"

A male voice interrupted her thoughts, dragging her back into her office and to reality.

Katrina spun around at the intrusion. She tossed a smile at Turk, one of the few men who worked at the office on her floor. He leaned his shoulder against the doorframe and grinned at her like he was a cat who had swallowed the canary.

"They always have the most irritating requests. We've done several properties for them and let me tell you, they're never happy."

"Oh," she laughed, "good. Then it's not me."

He moved farther into the room, shaking his head. "Nope. It's not. They can't make up their minds, and when they do, they hate it. Sometimes, you have to just put something completely different together and pray that they'll love it."

She made a face. "And what if they don't?"

Turk shrugged. "I've never been fired, so there's that."

Katrina laughed again. "Okay, fair enough." She turned back to the window and absentmindedly rolled the ball between her hands.

"I know that look." Turk came up beside her, though he didn't look in her direction.

"Yeah? What is it?"

His smile curled up at the ends. "You're homesick."

She snorted.

"You don't think so?" This time, he glanced toward her.

His light blue eyes and blond hair were a stark contrast to Simon's. Though they were striking, they didn't hold any allure for her at all. Turk had a reputation as being the flirtatious one at the company. But it didn't matter how sweet he was, Katrina wasn't interested.

Turk turned his attention to the window again. "You can be homesick and not miss your *home*. You could be homesick for a specific person. Or maybe it's a landmark. Or your family?"

He quirked a brow and shot one more look at her.

Simon's face flooded her thoughts. If there was anyone she was homesick for, it would be him.

"A guy. I knew it."

She jumped, turning startled eyes toward him. "I didn't say anything about a guy."

"You didn't have to."

She pressed her lips together firmly. Having people read her when they barely knew her wasn't something she appreciated, but then she didn't really have any say in the matter. "Whatever," she mumbled under her breath.

"For what it's worth, I think you made the right choice."

"Again," she forced a smile, "I didn't say anything. You have zero context for what you're saying."

He shrugged. "I work with a lot of women. I've dated them, I've broken up with them. Heck, I've been on the opposite side of the breakup more times than I can count. And *you* are pining for someone. But you're here now. So that means you made a choice. And I think you chose right."

"How would you know?" Her eyes narrowed and she frowned at him. "How can you possibly know what is good for me and what was the right choice? Because *I* barely know if I made the right choice. In fact, I'm pretty sure I've made the biggest mistake of my life."

Turk studied her for a moment, and it felt like he had managed to get past her defenses, all the walls she'd put up, everything that kept her safe before he finally spoke. "Easy. Because you wanted this. You wouldn't have come if you didn't. And people like you—the people who are willing to move away from friends and family—know exactly what they're doing. We're a special kind of breed—the ones who don't move our families with us. Granted, that's why most of us are single. The married ones are locals." He tossed her another flirty grin. "Give it some time. You'll see. One of these days everything will click, and you'll realize that this is where you were meant to be."

She watched him slip out of her office and disappear from view. Something about the way he'd tried to put everything into perspective didn't sit right with her. She couldn't tell if it was because the advice had come from a guy who clearly wanted to ask her out, or if it was because her gut was telling her that he couldn't be more wrong.

The rest of the workday dragged on much like the one before. Katrina found herself looking at the clock every hour or so, waiting for when she could take her leave—which was ridiculous when she wasn't all that thrilled to go home.

By the time the day was over and she arrived at her apartment, her feet were sore, her head ached, and she felt even more weighed down than before she'd taken the job in the first place. Her arms were loaded up with samples and books from her office, so she balanced everything just long enough to unlock the door and push it open with her foot.

With a groan, she dropped everything onto the table near the front door. Some of the magazines slipped to the floor, bringing her less-than-stellar day to an even worse end.

She sighed, dropping to her knees to gather the items just as her roommate emerged from the back. Becca was short with wavy brown hair. She'd said before that she hated her brown eyes and plain appearance, but Katrina thought she was beautiful. She could wear a pair of gym shorts and a baggy shirt and make it look chic.

Becca pulled open the fridge, glancing over her shoulder toward Katrina only briefly. "I thought when we got jobs, we didn't have to bring back homework."

Katrina huffed, placing her hands on her knees before grunting as she got to her feet. "Well, when you're the new girl and you're still learning the ropes, they sorta expect you to make the extra effort." She twisted around, facing Becca as she pulled a gallon of milk from the fridge. "And you should talk. What do you call all that?" She gestured sharply with one hand toward the stack of fifth-grade papers that littered the coffee table in the living room.

"That isn't homework."

Katrina snorted. "It's *literally* homework."

"Not *my* homework."

"Aren't you grading it?"

She glanced once more toward the stack of papers. "Nah. If they turned it in, I'm giving them points. It was an opinion paper, anyway."

"You're a lot nicer than my fifth-grade teacher."

Becca beamed. "Aw, you're sweet." She nodded toward the stack of stuff Katrina brought home. "What about yours? You didn't bring that stuff home last week or the week before."

"I've been a little… distracted."

Glass of milk in hand, Becca's eyes narrowed. "What's distracting you? It's not that guy, is it? The one who keeps hitting on you?"

"No... well, he did come into my office today. But he's not the distraction. I've been thinking a lot about why I'm here. And I just can't get something out of my head."

"What's that?" Becca returned the gallon jug to the fridge then took a sip of her beverage. "I thought you said you love your job. You like it here. All that fun stuff."

"I do like my job. And this place is exactly what I was looking for when I was job hunting. It's just... not the same."

Even from where Katrina stood on the other side of the room, she could see Becca's smile forming around the rim of her glass. "It's a guy, isn't it?"

Katrina rolled her eyes and turned toward her stack of what Becca affectionately referred to as homework. She avoided her roommate's inquisitive gaze. "Yeah. I guess it does all sorta stem from a guy."

"I knew it!" Becca practically hollered, making Katrina jump. I knew you were holding out on us. I knew you had a guy you were in love with."

Katrina could brush her off, tell her she was wrong and that this wasn't something she wanted to talk about. But the thought of having someone to confide in was just too nice to ignore. She didn't want to be alone in this anymore.

She sighed, tracing her finger along an image on a *Good Housekeeping* magazine. "He was my best friend growing up and... my biggest cheerleader."

"Ooh. This story is going to be good, I can already tell."

Katrina gave her a sad smile. "Unfortunately, it doesn't get a happily ever after. You might not like it as much as you think you will."

"Honey, the story isn't over."

"You don't know that."

"But I do. Love stories change, shift, and merge to form new stories. Whatever you're going through isn't as bad as you think it might be. And who knows? This guy you're about to tell me everything about could be thinking the very same thing. What if he doesn't want it to be over? What if he decides your story has a few more chapters to be written?"

"Don't let your tendency to romanticize things go to your head. He might have loved me once, but I assure you, he hates me now."

Becca put her cup down on the counter and crossed her arms, shaking her head for good measure. "Sorry, but you're wrong. While there is a thin line between love and hate, you can't simply cross that line whenever you want. If I had to guess, I would say that he's just hurt and when he gets his head on straight, you'll be hearing from him."

It was nice to have someone who wasn't quite so negative. Becca was a breath of fresh air and if Katrina wasn't careful, she'd end up making Brianne jealous of their newly formed friendship.

"Okay, okay. Sit down and I'll tell you the story of how my best friend made me fall in love with him and how I broke his heart."

Becca held up a hand. "Hold on. I think this calls for some popcorn. With extra butter." She winked at Katrina then hurried toward the pantry. "And then you can tell me how you're managing to steer clear of that guy at work."

CHAPTER TWENTY

Simon had become restless. There were no two ways about it. The more time he spent working his own farm—without Katrina—the more a certain realization weighed on him. As much as he loved this town, as much as he enjoyed owning the dairy farm, and as much as he wanted the horse training program to work, it wasn't the same without Katrina.

He'd stepped over the threshold from friendship to something more and he couldn't look back. His depressive state had gotten so bad that the only thing that made sense was to track her down and beg her to come home.

But how could he do that to her? He knew Katrina better than anyone. She wanted this job, wanted to be anywhere but here. If he asked her to come home, what did that say about him? It would say he was selfish, that's what. Eventually, she would resent him. Then he'd put up his walls and push her out.

Nothing good would come from him asking her to come home.

The only other option seemed equally terrible. He could sell the farm and move to the city to be with her. He had customer service experience. It wouldn't be hard to find a company willing to take him.

Just the thought of walking through a pair of doors to live the rest of his days working in a stuffy restaurant filled him with disgust. He'd gotten a taste of being able to live and work out in the open air.

He glanced around his property from the barn to the house. He loved it all—even the smells, which was saying something. There was only one question. Was he willing to give it all up if it meant he could be with Katrina?

That was the million-dollar question—one that Simon probably already knew the answer to. He just wasn't ready to act on it.

It was getting late, and the day had been grueling at best. Without Katrina around to break up the day with her smile, Simon had no other option but to dwell on what his life would be like without her.

A car pulled onto the property and from where he sat on the porch, he knew exactly who it was. Brianne had been visiting a lot more frequently lately despite his mood. It was becoming clearer and clearer that she was only trying to check up on him, and that irritated him even more.

She pulled her car to a stop, but he didn't bother getting up from where he was perched on the porch step. Simon didn't even look in her direction, hoping she'd take that as an indication of where he wanted this interaction to go.

Unfortunately, Brianne didn't seem to care much. She traipsed over to him and placed an envelope on his lap with a flourish. "You're welcome."

He glanced at the envelope, then swung his bored expression to Brianne. "I have plenty of envelopes, thanks," he muttered dryly.

"No, it's what's in the envelope."

"I don't really care what's in the envelope. I just want to enjoy looking out at everything that I can call my own," he said bitterly.

This was what he'd wanted, wasn't it? To have property, a place to call his own, something that was just for him and the start of his family. His heart was torn in two directions. The side of him that wanted this place was battling the side of him that wanted Katrina.

Hadn't he always felt that Rocky Ridge had only become a home to him because of the people who made it so? Katrina was one of those people. Brianne fit the bill too, but in a completely different way.

She was like that annoying little sister who got all the attention and tagged along wherever he went.

When he didn't immediately investigate the envelope contents, she snatched it from his lap and opened it, then withdrew a thick white piece of paper. "I'd start packing if I were you."

Simon turned his attention toward her. "What are you talking about?"

She waved the paper and envelope in front of his face, nearly hitting his nose. "Just look."

He yanked the paper from her hand and peered at it then his brows lifted. "This is an airplane ticket to Salt Lake City."

"Yep."

Slowly, Simon lifted his eyes to her. "It's for tomorrow."

"Yep."

He got to his feet. "This had to cost you a fortune. You can't just—"

"You remember that guy I was talking to the other day in town? He has some connections in the travel industry. I can't say what he did, exactly, but let's just say it wasn't as expensive as you might think." She beamed at him. "So get packed, go to Salt Lake City, and bring her home."

Simon shoved the ticket into Brianne's hand. "I can't."

"Yes. You can."

He shook his head. "I can't. Even if she wanted to see me, she definitely won't want to come back to Rocky Ridge. She's always wanted to live in the city, and you know it."

Brianne took his hand in hers and placed the envelope on it. "You have to try." Her smile widened slightly. "Besides, she called me the other day and she's miserable."

That was all he needed to hear to have his interest officially piqued. "Did she say that?"

She shook her head. "But I could hear it in her voice. I think she just needs an excuse to come home."

"She's got one. We all want her to come back."

"Not good enough. She needs a bigger reason—someone to come home to." Brianne's voice softened. "You two were great together, whether I want to admit it or not. So, get on that plane and do something about it before I completely lose it. Because, no offense, you haven't exactly been the best company around here lately."

"No offense taken," he mumbled, staring at the ticket in his hands. He couldn't believe he was considering this. Would Katrina even want to see him? Or would she think he was being overbearing?

When he glanced up, he found Brianne watching him. The grin she wore made it clear that she already thought she knew what was going to happen.

Simon sighed. "I don't have anyone who can help me out here—"

"Got that covered. Daniel said if I could convince you to go, he'd come by and make sure the place ran smoothly in your absence."

"Then I guess I don't have any other excuses."

"No, you don't."

∽

SIMON HELD up his phone one last time, checking that the address Katrina had given him was the same as the one in front of him. It was three in the afternoon, and he wasn't sure if she'd be home. He imagined her day ended around this time. She'd told him she went to work before the sun came up.

During the entirety of his flight, he hadn't been able to sit still. His thoughts were in an uproar, his heart beating at an unhealthy pace. He hadn't decided what he was going to tell her yet. Did he beg her to come back to the town she hated for him? For her family?

Or did he tell her that he didn't care where she decided to put down roots; he would be willing to give up everything he had if it meant he could be with her.

The latter seemed like a more likely option. He'd never be one to make demands like that. But he also knew he was capable of fighting for what he truly wanted.

He lifted his chin, determination ripping through him like a heavy storm. This was his only shot and he wasn't going to squander it. Katrina would know exactly where he stood. He might have told her to chase her dreams—and he didn't regret it—but he should have done everything he could to keep her, too.

Simon climbed the steps to the third floor of the building, The steps wrapped around a corner to where a set of doors faced a balcony. There were two apartments on this side, and the one with the big, bold letter 'A' would be the one that opened up his world of opportunity.

He lifted his hand and knocked firmly on the door then stepped back.

A sudden surge of nerves slipped away the moment the door opened. "Katrina, I wanted to…"

His voice trailed off as he got a good look at the young woman who'd opened the door. Her hazel eyes and wavy brown hair didn't belong to the woman he loved.

His face flushed and he let out a strangled chuckle. "Sorry, I... does Katrina live here?"

The woman smiled, leaning against the door as she did. "Yes, may I ask who you are?"

He tugged at his collar and glanced away. "I'm a friend from back home."

"A *friend*?" Her teasing smile caused all those nerves to return with a vengeance. "Maybe I've heard of you. What's your name?"

Simon swallowed hard and pushed through his worries. He was here, wasn't he? There was no turning back. He attempted to look around the woman but then gave up with a sigh.

"My name's Simon."

There was a brief recognition in her eyes—something that seemed to confirm what she'd said. Katrina had talked about him.

"Look, I'm not going to be in town for very long and I'd really like to have a word with her. I'd like to spend as much time as I can with her while I'm here." He shifted to the side to get a better look at the apartment behind this woman in hopes of catching sight of the one he'd come here to see, but failed.

Katrina's roommate adjusted her stance, too, continuing to block his view. "I'm sorry, but she's not going to be home for another couple hours."

"Hours?"

She nodded. "Sure. The people at that company have got her wrapped around their finger. I don't think I've seen anyone work so hard to please their boss as Katrina does."

"Yeah, well, that's Katrina for you."

She shifted her weight from one foot to the other, her eyes trailing up and down his form. "I have to say, you're nothing like I expected."

"Oh? Why is that?"

She laughed, the sound a soft tinkling one that probably got a lot of attention from interested men. "Well, you're not wearing a cowboy hat, for one." She gestured toward his feet. "But those boots are on point."

He glanced at his feet, lifting one about half an inch from the ground before replacing it. "Yeah, well, it's not ideal to fly in a plane with a cowboy hat."

"No, I don't suppose it is."

"And I'm still getting used to them."

Her smile creeped wider across her face. "Katrina did mention something to that effect." She tilted her head, resting her cheek against the door itself. "If you'd like, you can stay here until she gets home."

"I don't think that will be necessary." His plan B had been to go hunting for a company that had a business name resembling what he thought Katrina had said.

"Or I can give you the address for her office. I'm sure she could take fifteen minutes to talk to you if it's that important."

His eyes cut to meet hers, drilling into her to determine if she were telling the truth. He found no evidence that she had any interest in lying. Shoving his phone in her direction, he pointed to the screen. "That sounds great. I'd like to put it in my maps app so I can go straight there."

She laughed again, shaking her head as she accepted his device. "It's not far from here. If you go down to that main cross street about two blocks from here, then you'll turn left and stay on the sidewalk until you arrive." She tapped the screen with finality and handed it back. "I'm Becca, by the way."

"Nice to meet you." Simon reached up to touch his hat, then recalled the conversation they'd had regarding the lack thereof.

Becca's smile seemed to be more humorous this time, like she was laughing at him. It didn't matter. He had the address, and he would likely not see her again for the rest of his life. What did it matter if she was making fun of him?

He gave her one more nod and hurried down the steps toward the parking lot. Based on what Becca had said, Katrina would be working until around five. He had plenty of time just so long as he made it to the right floor and past security.

The closer he got to the building, the calmer he felt, which was strange. Maybe this was his heart and mind finally coming to an agreement. He was on the right track, and he was going to come out of this on top.

CHAPTER TWENTY-ONE

Katrina bit her bottom lip as she stood across from her supervisor—the person who'd had the final say in hiring her. Kendall was a great boss. Katrina had nothing against her or anyone at the firm, but she had finally realized that somewhere between losing her job in California and getting the one here in Salt Lake, her priorities had changed.

The hardest part was that this could mean the end of working in this particular industry. There was no way Kendall would give her a good recommendation now. And Katrina couldn't blame her.

Kendall hadn't looked up from the document in her hand —the letter of resignation that Katrina had painfully put together late into the night. Katrina knew better than to believe it was taking her this long to read through the whole thing. She'd probably figured out exactly what it was when she'd read the first line.

And still, Kendall was taking her time with a response.

Katrina shifted, fidgeted, and nearly ran from the office. She had never quit a job she liked so much. But since her heart simply wasn't in it, she couldn't rationalize staying.

Clearing her throat, she shifted again. "Like I said, I'm so sorry."

Kendall's eyes bounced up to meet hers. "Yes, you did say that."

Great, she was disappointed. Her voice practically dripped with it. Why was it so hard for Katrina to disappoint the people she worked with?

Pushing down that ugly feeling as far as it would go, Katrina forced a smile. "I really did love working here, but it's not working."

Her supervisor lifted one brow and put the letter on her desk. When she steepled her fingers, Katrina almost felt like she could see right through her—down to her soul. She knew. She knew that Katrina was giving up a great job for a guy.

Not even a guy!

She was giving up a great job because she wanted the *chance* to be with a guy she had no guarantee would even take her back.

But she had to try.

"You know, we have a special program here—one where we will take on remote workers under special circumstances."

Katrina's whole body stiffened.

Kendall's smirk might have grated against Katrina's nerves if her boss hadn't just dropped this bomb on her. Remotely working for this company would be the solution to all of her problems. If she could manage that, then she might just get to have everything she ever wanted. Well, as long as Simon would give her a chance.

When Katrina finally found her voice, she blurted, "Is that something you could offer me?"

"Me?" She laughed. "No, it's above my paygrade. You're still new, and usually they don't offer this sort of thing to rookies."

Katrina's heart dropped. Why dangle the carrot if it wasn't something she could do?

"That being said," Kendall drawled, "I'm sure I could pass this on to my boss with a note that suggests we can't let you slip through our fingers."

"You'd do that?" Katrina blurted, stepping forward. She flushed, snapping her mouth shut. "I'm sorry."

Kendall leaned back in her office chair, making it creak just a little. "Don't think that I haven't noticed you've been a little distracted."

Uh-oh. That didn't sound good.

"But your work is still on par with those who have been working here for at least five years, if not more. The way I see it, keeping you on would be a better investment than looking for someone new."

"Thank you. I really appreciate your feedback." While on the outside, Katrina was doing her best at keeping her cool, on the inside she was screaming with joy.

"Of course, there's no guarantee that they will go for it, but with your latest project and my recommendation, I think you stand a good chance." Kendall got to her feet and held out the letter of resignation. "I'm sorry to see you go. But before you do anything official, please let me send a few emails."

Katrina nodded, accepting the document. "I can do that."

She left the office feeling like she could conquer the world. She turned the corner to her office so quickly that she collided with a tall body, dropping her letter of resignation to the ground.

She gasped and crouched down, but he was faster. He scooped up her letter and that was when she recognized the boots. As they both stood, her eyes darted to Simon's face and her heart stopped.

"Simon?" Her voice cracked. "What are you doing here?"

He stared at the document in his hand, brows furrowed. Then his eyes flitted back to meet hers and he held it up. "What's this?"

Her instincts told her to snatch it out of his hands and brush it off. She hadn't figured out what she wanted to tell him regarding her decision to come home, and now it was back to being up in the air.

No, not in the air. She still planned on leaving. It was whether the company wanted to keep her or cut her loose that could change. She smiled apprehensively, opting to look at the paper instead of his scrutinizing eyes. "It's a letter of resignation."

"I know that. But why do you have it?"

"It's mine."

"You know what I'm trying to ask," he whispered. His hand dropped to his side, and he raked his free one through his hair so haphazardly that it left him looking like he'd just climbed out of bed. "You know what? Never mind. I came here to tell you something and that's what I'm going to do." He straightened his shoulders and leaned forward so he could take one of her hands in his.

"Simon, you don't have to—"

"Let me just say my piece, okay? I've gone over it and over it in my head and I'll never forgive myself if I don't get it out." He took a deep breath and then sighed. "The farm is just a place. What I have there? They're just things, just possessions. I can't take any of that with me into the next life, but I *can* take my memories. I *can* take my heart."

Her own heart had burst into overdrive at his words, but he wasn't prepared to give her a turn to speak.

"There's only one thing that makes sense to me—one thing that is more important than anything else. And that's family. All I know is that family is going to be the thing that gets me through. Family will be the one part of my life that will both heal my heart and make it happy. Katrina, my heart belongs to you."

Mouth dry, lump in her throat, Katrina couldn't bring herself to utter a single syllable. Heck, she probably couldn't even mumble without sounding like a little mouse. He was saying everything she should have said when she was deciding whether to take this job. Hand it to Simon to be the brave one, the generous one, the one who had managed to change her heart without her realizing it.

Katrina threw her arms around his neck and peppered his face with kisses. When she pulled back, her nose and cheeks were flushed not only from the kiss but from the utter embarrassment over what she'd done. Yet again, she'd put what she'd thought she wanted at the forefront of her mind.

The funny thing was that her job here wasn't important anymore. She reached down and took the paper from his hand. "Give me one second."

Katrina hurried the few steps back to her boss's office, marched right up to her desk and put the letter front and center.

"I appreciate what you're trying to do for me, and if it works out, that's great. But one way or another, my last day in the office will be two weeks from now."

She didn't even bother waiting for Kendall to give her a response before she took off.

Once she was out the door and into the hallway, she all but threw herself at Simon. "I can't believe you came," she murmured. "I don't think you've ever been out of Rocky Ridge."

"I haven't," he murmured.

"And you came all this way…"

"To tell you I love you and I'm not going to stand by and let you walk out of my life."

She tilted her head and smiled. "And what would you have done if I told you that I'm not coming back?"

"I thought that was clear." The lines in his brow deepened. "I would go anywhere to be with you, Katrina. You are my home."

Her heart fluttered again. "Well, lucky for both of us, I've realized something, too."

He waited, his boyish grin fueling her like nothing else could.

"I can't stand the city anymore." Before he could misunderstand her statement, she inched closer and lowered her voice. "It's not *really* the city or the people. It's a lot more than that." She dug deep, hoping what she had to say would resonate with him the way his words had with her. "Honestly? I think if I knew you could be happy here, I'd stay—just so long as I had you."

He blinked. "Well, that's an option—"

"No, it's not. You'd be absolutely miserable if we stayed here. You would hate the traffic, the noises, and the crime. Heck, I would wager that you'd even hate the fact that people here wouldn't know your name." Katrina laughed, then her expression sobered and she placed a hand to his cheek before pushing it up into his hair and letting her fingers feather through the strands. "You have spent your whole life being there for me—the only one I could count on to always be by my side. You've only ever wanted my happiness." Her emotions got the better of her, and her voice shook slightly. "It's my turn to make sure you find your happiness."

"I am happy—"

She shook her head. "I mean really happy, Simon. The way you felt when you found out you got to keep the farm. The way you felt when you signed that paperwork with Megan and Daniel. Those were moments in your life that you will never forget. They're such a part of your core, I could never ask you to leave them behind."

Here she was, putting her heart out on the line. Yes, there was less risk involved after he'd taken charge and told her exactly how he felt. But that didn't change the fact that she felt one hundred percent vulnerable in this very moment. She was so humbled by it all that she couldn't find the words she really wanted to say.

"Hey, why are you crying?"

She blinked and another tear slipped down her cheek. "So I am," she murmured, wiping at her cheek with her fingertips. "I'm just so… happy." She forced a smile, but Simon wasn't having any of it.

"That doesn't look like a happy smile."

"It is," she insisted. "These are happy tears. And there's only one thing I have left to do."

"What's that?" His arms tightened around her waist, and he pressed his forehead against hers. "What are you going to do?"

Katrina let out a sad little laugh. "I need you to forgive me. I can't believe I let my selfish impulses drive my decisions.

I want you to know that I'm going to change. I'm going to take more responsibility and make choices that will benefit us both." She placed her hand to his cheek again. "We both deserve to be happy."

"Amen," he murmured, tilting her chin upward.

"Does this mean you'll forgive me?" she rasped as he drew closer.

His hot breath grazed her face. "You didn't even have to ask."

His lips captured Katrina's, stealing her breath and making it incredibly difficult to stay balanced on her own two legs. She leaned into him, giving her whole spirit to their future together.

Something that at one time had felt outrageous was now the one thing that made sense. Simon was her best friend. He knew her inside and out. He loved her more than anyone else.

Katrina was the first to break the kiss as the world around them came back into focus. Several of her co-workers were giving them incredulous looks and she let out a quiet laugh. "I guess it's a good thing I won't be working here anymore. I don't think I'd hear the end of this."

His mouth quirked upward at the corners. "You're probably right."

She reached for his hand. "I love you. I'm so glad you came."

"Me too," he murmured before kissing her temple. "Now I just have to figure out where I'm going to stay for the next day or so." He squeezed her hand. "Even if there was room at your place, I don't think it'd be wise to spend another moment with Becca."

Katrina laughed. "She's harmless. She might talk a little too much, but she's actually a really good friend. You know what? I'm going to see if I can get off early today so I can show you around. How does that sound?"

"I think it sounds perfect."

CHAPTER TWENTY-TWO

Six months later

Time had flown by since the afternoon when Simon had poured his heart out to Katrina. Hindsight being what it was, he shouldn't have been so nervous.

Well, not as nervous as he was today. Because this evening, he had something big planned.

Never in a million years did Simon think his life would get to this point. Katrina had always just been that friend who made him feel special. She had been the one to assure him that he was where he was always meant to be.

It wasn't that he was worried Katrina would turn him down. He had more confidence in their relationship than ever before. No, his nerves stemmed from his desire to ensure everything was perfect. She had given up so much to be with him, from leaving her corporate job in the city to moving to a place where she never wanted to end up—he wanted to make sure she was happy.

Most importantly, he wanted to make sure she was happy with him.

His whole body was on edge. And while he was supposed to be focused on the meeting at hand, he couldn't seem to pay attention.

"Simon, are you with us?"

He snapped his head up and stared at Daniel. "Yes, of course."

Daniel glanced from Simon to the handful of other men who were now working for him. Their training business had exploded, which meant additional hands were needed to keep the dairy farm running. And since Daniel was part owner of the training program, he insisted on having weekly meetings. It was probably something that had carried over from when he owned the coffee shop in town.

A sly smile stole across Daniel's face before he continued. "Like I was saying, we need to be prepared for the fair this weekend. We have two booths set up—one for each side of the business. I will be stopping in to check on things, but my wife will also have a booth for the bookstore, and she's requested I stay close by in case she needs help." Daniel's eyes landed on Simon and he nodded.

Simon shifted, glancing around the group.

Daniel sighed. "Simon will be handing out assignments. Even though most of you work the dairy farm side of things, some of you will be asked to man the training table. This will be an opportunity for you to show your stuff in case you'd like to be considered for a job change."

Oh, right. Simon was supposed to give that tidbit of information. He dropped his eyes to the ground and twisted his heel into the dirt. Daniel was bound to notice that he hadn't been on top of things the last couple of days. Simon could see a talk in the near future—one he wasn't ready to have with his future brother-in-law.

The second the group broke up to do their chores, Simon did the same—only he chose to dart for the house. If he could get into his office, then he had a good chance of being "too busy" to talk to Daniel.

"Simon."

He froze.

"A word."

Dang it!

Slowly, Simon turned to face his business partner. "What do you need, Daniel? Seems to me we have everything all squared away."

Daniel lifted a brow, moving toward him like a predator. "You've been... distracted lately."

"Have I?"

The flat look Daniel shot him was enough to make Simon think a little harder about avoiding this discussion. "You have, and if you're not careful, that distraction is going to get you in trouble. This business might be thriving, but it won't always be like that. You need to do everything you can to make it the best it can be now so when we fall on hard times, we have some cushion."

Simon let his focus sweep over the farm surrounding them. Even after all this time, it still felt like a dream. His life had changed so much, and it was only getting better with each passing day.

He turned his attention back to Daniel. "I'm not an idiot. I know that we need to plan for the worst. I'm just…" He rubbed the back of his neck then dropped his hand to his side. "I'm just trying to figure something out."

"Anything I can help with?"

His gaze cut to Daniel. "No. I think I'm good."

"So not business, then."

"Not business."

Daniel's frown remained. "Does it have to do with Katrina?"

The look on his face must have given him away in a second, because Daniel's brows popped up and he grinned.

"You're going to ask her to marry you, aren't you?" Daniel smacked his forehead with his palm. "I can't believe I didn't see it before. Katrina mentioned you two had a date tonight." He moved forward and his heavy hand landed on Simon's shoulder. "Congratulations!"

"Thanks, but it hasn't happened yet."

"Is that what you're worried about? You know Katrina is crazy about you, right? She's going to say yes."

"I know that." Simon sighed. "I just want to make sure it's what she wants. I don't want her settling for something she doesn't want."

Daniel sobered. "Katrina loves you. She's not going to regret anything."

"I get that. But she still had to quit a job she was excited about so she could come back to be here with me. There's just this…"

"I'm not going to say you shouldn't worry. Because that's just part of being human. But I want you to consider one thing. She'd decided to quit before you showed up. She wanted to come back. If she was going to resent anyone, it would have to be herself. She made this choice."

"That doesn't mean she can't have a certain level of remorse for making that choice. What if one day she wakes up and wishes things were different?"

"Then I guess you'll deal with it when you get to that point. For now, live in the moment. Believe me, it's more important to find your happiness wherever you can get it because nothing is set in stone." Daniel clapped his hand on Simon's shoulder once more and headed away.

He was right. There was no telling how easy or hard life would be, but as long as he and Katrina were together, that was all that mattered.

∽

KATRINA HOVERED by the front window, waiting for Simon to show up for their date. She'd just gotten the most amazing news and the only person she wanted to share it with was Simon. She could barely stand still as she waited. Her weight continued to shift from one foot to the other in a little nervous dance.

The second he pulled up in front of her house, she darted outside. The words nearly tumbled from her lips, but for some reason, she held back. She wanted the moment to be right. This was a big step for her—for both of them. She was basically telling him that she was choosing to stay here indefinitely. There was nothing else calling to her and nothing would make her happier than to be in Rocky Ridge with the man she loved.

Simon opened her door, and she climbed inside. The whole way to their destination, he was quiet. She couldn't explain it, but she got the sense that he was lost in thought—far away somewhere.

For no other reason than the fact that her own insecurities had clawed themselves free of the prison where she'd kept them, Katrina's thoughts turned to the worst-case scenario. Was he realizing that they weren't supposed to be together? What if he thought he'd made a mistake in coming to Salt Lake to win her back?

By the time they pulled into the parking lot, she wasn't so sure whether she should tell him her news. But all it took was one glance in his direction and she knew that if she didn't tell him how she felt, how happy she was, she'd regret it. Whether they stayed together or drifted apart, Simon needed to know the effect he had on her.

She opened her mouth and they both spoke. "Simon—"

"Katrina—"

Shutting her mouth, she contemplated if she should let him speak first. But if she was right in her concerns, then her announcement wouldn't hit the way it should. "Can I go first?"

Simon nodded.

She smiled nervously, facing him and taking his hand in both of hers. "I got some pretty great news today."

His brows lifted slightly.

"You know how I asked that company in Salt Lake if they would take me on as a remote worker?"

He nodded. "But I thought they turned you down."

"They did," she hurried on, "but they have a sister company that was working out some hiring issues and they sent my information over to them. I guess they were finally able to review my application because they finally got back to me." Katrina bit down on her lower lip, the surge of excitement returning. "I can't believe it, but they want me to work for them. From wherever I live."

His eyes widened.

"I know! This is perfect. I get to stay here, in Rocky Ridge —with my family, and Brianne…" She inched closer, and her voice lowered. "And with you."

Simon blinked and looked away, his brows coming together. This was it. This was the look she was so concerned about. He didn't want to be in a relationship anymore. She could already hear his confession in her head.

"Are you sure that's what you want?" Simon's voice was low, weak sounding, even. It rasped with that sort of finality that she despised.

"Yes," she said firmly, still holding tight to his hand. She waited for him to look in her direction before she continued. "I've spent my whole life chasing dream after dream without realizing why none of them were fulfilling me the way they should have been. I realized in Salt Lake City that I was chasing the wrong ones."

Simon's expression was unreadable. If only she could see a glimmer of something that could ease her troubled heart. Unfortunately, he was holding his cards much too close to his chest.

"We've been here for six months, and I don't have any regrets." She ducked her head, emphasizing the next word. *"Zero."*

Her heart beat like shutters against the house during a raging storm. It thundered and cracked as she drew on what little courage she had left to tell Simon where she stood.

"This place has always been home. I was just too blind to see it. And you were always meant to be mine." Her voice cracked on the last word as she swallowed back the emotion that threatened to overwhelm her. "I'm not going anywhere, Simon. This is where I'm meant to be."

Finally, she saw a hint of a smile touch his lips, and a burst of butterflies exploded in her chest. Perhaps she still had a chance.

"Simon, I wanted to ask you something—"

He held up his free hand. "Don't."

She choked back the next few words she was going to say and her whole body went stiff.

"You have always known what you wanted, where you wanted to be, and who you wanted to spend your time with. You were always the brave one, shooting for the stars with everything you did." Simon placed his hand over the top of hers then looked down at them. "I've always admired that about you. You were always the person I wanted to be like."

Katrina bit back a surprised laugh. "I wasn't—"

"Let me finish."

She blinked, closing her mouth again.

"At the same time, I was always willing to step back and let you do your thing. And it was always worth it. Until now."

Her heart stumbled.

"Katrina, I can't go on living a life where you are the one who charges into the mist to go after what you want. I can count on one hand how often I have done the same, and today I'm going to add to that list." He chuckled then shook his head. "I really didn't want my truck to be the place where we did this, but you gave me no choice."

Simon reached into his pocket and withdrew something she couldn't see. He had it in the palm of his hand and when she dragged her gaze from his hand to his face, she was startled to find his eyes shining with an intensity she'd never seen before.

"I'm done being a coward who lets his life pass him by. I'm tired of being the bystander. Today, I'm going to put my heart on the line and tell you that there's no one else but you. There's no one I would rather spend the rest of my life with than you."

Tears of relief and joy brimmed in her eyes, and she blinked furiously to clear them away.

"I couldn't have said it better myself."

He grinned. His hand opened, revealing a modest engagement ring—a single stone on a gold band. It was absolutely perfect.

Katrina gasped and looked up into Simon's adoring gaze.

"Will you marry me?"

"You didn't even have to ask," she murmured. Katrina wrapped her arms around his neck in an awkward hug and they both laughed.

Simon pulled back first. "You know, it wouldn't hurt if we got out of the truck and I did it proper."

She gave him a strange look. "What?"

Simon lifted a shoulder. "Nothing, I just figured you deserved to have the most perfect proposal and usually that entails the man getting down on one knee."

Katrina laughed again but sobered when she realized he was serious. "Simon, this *was* the perfect proposal. Because you were the one who asked me."

"And you said yes."

She nodded and pulled him closer so she could press her forehead to his. "I said yes."

EPILOGUE

Simon sat at a large table that had been made up of several smaller tables out behind the Reese's home. Apparently, barbecues were a normal occurrence during the summer nowadays—something Katrina had neglected to tell him.

He didn't mind. In fact, being with her family this way was still taking a lot of getting used to. While he'd grown up with Katrina and spent a great deal of his time with her at her home, he hadn't spent a lot of time with her brothers. And now that each of them was married and starting a family, this "little" barbecue was turning out to be much bigger than he'd expected.

His eyes bounced from one person to the next as they all chatted and filled in the rest of the family on what was new.

Katrina took his hand in hers and he met her gaze. Her smile was all it took to settle his nerves. This was what it felt like to be part of a family—something he hadn't experienced since he was a child. It was terrifying at times, but more than that, it was absolutely exhilarating, and he couldn't wait for the day when he'd be able to say he was officially part of it.

"So, Katrina, what's the plan for the wedding? Will you be getting married in a church? The back yard? A reception center?"

Katrina glanced toward one of her sisters-in-law. "Well, I was thinking—"

"Actually," Simon cut in, drawing all eyes toward him. He swallowed hard, not prepared for all the attention. "Actually," he tried again, "it was supposed to be a surprise, but I've been holding onto some of my inheritance for a special occasion and I wanted to give Katrina the opportunity for a destination wedding."

There were gasps, and eyes that widened so far he was sure people were going to lose their sight. But it was the shock that mingled with excitement that was written all over Katrina's face that he cared about most.

His voice softened and he took her hand into both of his. "You've always had a love of far-off places. You've been all over the country, and I wanted to make sure you knew you could continue chasing those experiences—just so long as you do so with me."

Some of the woman sighed, and Simon could have sworn one or two of the men groaned. But none of that mattered as long as Katrina liked that idea.

"What do you say? Want to go on an adventure with me?"

The strangled sound that escaped her lips didn't sound happy at all, but the look of adoration on her face was enough to clear that up. "I don't want you to think you have to fill some kind of box. I love you. I will always love you, no matter what. No regrets."

He pressed his head to hers, something they had a tendency to do when they really wanted something to hit home. "No regrets," he repeated.

Katrina glanced around the table. "What do you guys think? Because this isn't just about Simon and me. This is about our whole family. Each and every one of us." She set her eyes on each individual at the table, and Simon watched as they all nodded and smiled. This family was a shining example of what could happen when a family supported each other and built one another up. Katrina rested her cheek against Simon's chest. "I can't wait."

"Have you thought about who you want to be your bridesmaids? What about the groomsmen?" Katrina's mother asked.

Simon glanced down at his fiancée with a wide smile. "I think it would only make sense to have my future brothers be the ones to support me when I stand in front of everyone and promise myself to my wife."

Katrina grinned. Then she glanced around the table. "I already promised Brianne and Becca that they could be part of the wedding party. I'm so sorry. I can't have all of you."

Megan laughed. "It's definitely not my scene. I don't like the frou-frou dresses or heels. But if you want a coordinator, I'm pretty good at that."

One of the other sisters he couldn't remember the name of nodded her agreement. "I'll pass, too." She gestured toward her growing belly. "I'd rather stay off my feet if possible. Everything is only going to continue to get more swollen."

A few of the other ladies chuckled.

"Then that settles it. Emily and Julia will be my other bridesmaids." Katrina snuggled closer to him and let out a contented sigh. "And who knows? Maybe this will be just the event for my other friends to find their true loves."

Simon laughed. "I don't think Brianne is interested in settling down just yet."

Katrina shrugged. "You never know." She straightened. "Oh, that reminds me. Mom, Becca has the summer off and she was hoping to come stay with us before the wedding. Can she use the guest room?"

"I'm sorry, sweetie, your cousin Ethan will be helping out on the ranch this summer. We've already offered the room to him."

"He can stay with the other stable hands in the wranglers' cabin," Bo murmured. "He'd probably prefer it that way, anyway. I don't think he's gonna want to have to deal with all the wedding planning going on." He passed a knowing look with one of his brothers.

"Then it's settled," Katrina chirped. "Becca stays with us in the house and Ethan gets to be in the cabin." She gave

Simon a loving look, one he knew he'd never tire of. "And you and I can start planning our lives together."

"Here in Rocky Ridge," he murmured.

"Right where we both belong," she agreed.

∼

MORE FROM APRIL MURDOCK

Sagebrush Ranch

When You're Friends
When You're Waiting
When You're His Crush
When You're Competing
When You're Finally Home
When You're Fake Dating
When You're Enemies
When You're Keeping Secrets

Returning to Rocky Ridge

One Last Chance
Two Cowboy Promises
Three Times Charmed

Billionaire Ranchers Second Generation

Faking Her Engagement

MORE FROM APRIL MURDOCK

Protecting His Heart
Marrying Her Friend
Dating Her Crush
Taking His Chance
Trusting Her Hero

The Brothers of Duncan Ranch

A Party Planner for the Cowboy
A Second Chance for the Cowboy
A Rare Beauty for the Cowboy
An Open Heart for the Cowboy
A Christmas Kiss for the Cowboy

Silverstone Dude Ranch

Cowboy's Redemption
Cowboy's Surprise
Cowboy's Competition
Cowboy's Fate
Cowboy's Challenge
Cowboy's Assumption
Cowboy's Myth
Cowboy's Rival
Cowboy's Destiny

Billionaire Ranchers Series

Impressing Her Billionaire Cowboy Boss
Keeping Her Billionaire Cowboy CEO
Saving Her Billionaire Cowboy Hero
Loving Her Billionaire Cowboy Partner
Arguing With Her Billionaire Cowboy

MORE FROM APRIL MURDOCK

Teaching Her Billionaire Cowboy Rookie

The Brothers of Thatcher Ranch

The Cowboy's One and Only
The Cowboy's City Girl
The Cowboy's Troublemaker
The Cowboy's Second Chance

Wealth and Kinship

The Billionaire's Heart
The Billionaire's Hope
The Billionaire's Generosity
The Billionaire's Loyalty
The Billionaire's Sincerity
The Billionaire's Promise

Silverstone Ranch

The Movie Star Becomes a Cowboy
The Cowboy gets a Second Chance
The Chef Chases His Cowboy Dream
The Billionaire Tries the Cowboy Life
The Royal Cowboy Chooses Love

Texas Redemption

A Long Road Home for the Broken Ranger
Sweet Second Chances for the Reluctant Billionaire
New Inspiration for the Lonely Rockstar
A Change of Plans for the Youngest Son
A Rude Awakening for the Ambitious Ex-Boyfriend

MORE FROM APRIL MURDOCK

Small Town Billionaires

The Billionaire's High School Reunion
The Aimless Billionaire
The Billionaire's Charity Date
The Beach Bum Billionaire
The Grouchy Billionaire
The Billionaire's Home Town

Christmas Miracles

Her Undercover Billionaire Boss
The Billionaire's Family Christmas
Christmas Carols for the Billionaire

Made in the USA
Middletown, DE
15 July 2024